Wolf Man

BOOKS BY EDO VAN BELKOM

Wolf Pack
Lone Wolf
Cry Wolf
Wolf Man

Be Afraid!
Be Very Afraid!

Wolf Man

EDO VAN BELKOM

Tundra Books

Published in Canada by Tundra Books,
75 Sherbourne Street, Toronto, Ontario M5A 2P9

Published in the United States by Tundra Books of Northern New York,
P.O. Box 1030, Plattsburgh, New York 12901

Library of Congress Control Number: 2007938539

Library and Archives Canada Cataloguing in Publication

Van Belkom, Edo
Wolf man / Edo van Belkom.

ISBN 978-0-88776-819-4

1. Werewolves – Fiction. I. Title.

PS8593.A53753W637 2008 jC813'.54 C2007-906098-6

We acknowledge the financial support of the Government of Canada through the Book Publishing Industry Development Program (BPIDP) and that of the Government of Ontario through the Ontario Media Development Corporation's Ontario Book Initiative. We further acknowledge the support of the Canada Council for the Arts and the Ontario Arts Council for our publishing program.

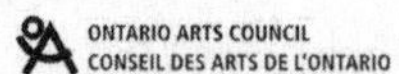

Typeset in Plantin
Printed and bound in Canada

This book is printed on acid-free paper that is 100% recycled, ancient-forest friendly (40% post-consumer recycled).

1 2 3 4 5 6 13 12 11 10 09 08

To Shaun Ellis, a true wolf man

Prologue

The wolves had been through this part of the forest so many times, they'd worn a path through the trees. On their previous travels, they'd moved from bush to tree to bush without a sound, without disturbing branches, and without letting any other being in the forest know they were there.

But not on this night.

Tonight they followed their leader, who boldly strode between the trees brushing aside branches and stomping saplings beneath him like so much deadwood. The pack's alpha male didn't try to hide his presence, but instead moved as if announcing his existence to the world and proclaiming his rule over all that surrounded him.

In the past, the pack would be cautious around the places of men, scurrying from shadow to shadow for fear they might be caught where they did not belong.

Some men were good and worthy of respect, and the wolves knew where they lived and how to find them. Other men, however, were bad and killed without reason. They were also weak, but they had cowardly ways of making themselves strong – ways to kill without touch, tooth, or claw.

Deathsticks! That's what they were like, and sometimes all it took was for a man with one of those sticks to see you. Then there would be a loud *crack*, or a *boom* that echoed down the mountain, and just like that, something would be dead.

Alive one moment, dead the next.

That's what men could do.

And so the pack feared men and had learned to stay away from them, venturing near their dens and lairs only when there was no other choice, even then only at night and only in silence.

But not on this night.

Tonight they would go to the places where men lived.

It was dangerous, to be sure, but they really had no choice.

While the icy chill of Mother Earth had made it hard for the wolves to survive – much of their prey hiding beneath a blanket of snow – men still had food . . . more than they could ever eat.

And so the wolves moved from place to place in search of easy prey, hunting the animals that belonged to men, or maybe even the men themselves.

After all, it was only fair.

No, more than just fair, it was *right*.

Nature's way.

Because while the wolves of the pack moved through the forest on four legs, their leader now walked on two.

He had fought a man-wolf, nearly to the death, but he had survived and grown stronger. Now he was one of them. He was still *wolf* – of that, there was no doubt – but he was also part *man*, and if he were man, then those things belonging to men should be his as well.

He would take what he needed.

And when he did, Mother Earth help the man who got in his way.

Chapter 1

Ernie Ilson pushed a fresh log into the potbellied stove in his living room, then turned the crank at the bottom of the stove to clear the ashes that had accumulated at the base of the fire. The last week had been bitterly cold up on the mountain, and the stove had been going pretty much around the clock. In the morning, he'd have to clean out the ashes and make a few trips to the woodpile by the shed to restock his supply of firewood. But that was work for tomorrow. Right now, it was Ernie's job to relax. He'd had a fine supper – thanks to his good friend Captain High Liner – tomorrow's lunch was in the bag, and breakfast was already laid out on the kitchen table. All that remained was for him to sit back in his favorite chair, read the evening paper awhile, then nap til it was time to go to bed. Then, in the morning, Ernie's life cycle would begin all over again.

Satisfied the fire would be all right for the next hour, Ernie closed the door on the stove and trudged over to his well-worn La-Z-Boy. He picked up the copy of the *Redstone Gazette* that lay on the seat and read the big bold headline splashed across the front page – PROVINCE COMMENDS REDSTONE TEEN FOR FOREST RESCUE.

"Did you see that?" he asked.

No one answered Ernie's question because there was no one else in the room. No one else except for Jaeger, his golden retriever. The two had been together eight years now, helping each other through some pretty tough times, including the death of Ernie's wife six years ago to cancer. When she passed, it looked for a while like Ernie might join her, but Jaeger pulled him through the dark times by keeping him active and forcing him to go for walks at least three times a day. After a few months, the worst of the pain had passed and the two of them became constant companions.

Man, and man's best friend.

Ernie turned the paper around so Jaeger, who was curled up on the rug next to the chair, could see. "That's one of them Brock kids," he said. "The biggest one of the three boys . . . name of Argyle, or. . . ," he scanned the newspaper article, "yeah, Argus, that's it. Strong boy, not the best-looking kid – looks a bit like you, Jaeger, but bigger. Much bigger."

Jaeger responded by raising his head slightly and letting out a sound that was halfway between a *groan* and a *chuff.* That was one of the things Ernie liked most about Jaeger – he was easy to talk to. Not like the previous dog, Hanna, who'd been his wife's dog and not much of a conversationalist.

Ernie sat down in his chair, eased it back into a reclining position, and read further about how Argus, with the help of his brother and sister, had found a lost girl in the forest and brought her all the way to the hospital in Redstone, probably saving her life.

"Well, good for him," Ernie said aloud. Then he leaned right, to speak to Jaeger. "I always thought they were strange kids. You know, like there was something *off* about them . . . but then they go and rescue some lost kid in the forest." He sniffed. "I guess they can't be all bad, eh, Jaeger?"

Jaeger barked.

"Easy, boy," Ernie said. "When I said they can't be *all* bad, that means they're *good*."

But Jaeger barked again.

Ernie put down the paper, concerned now because the dog wasn't usually so chatty. "What is it?"

The dog got up off the rug and looked toward the rear door.

"You hear something, Jaeger? What's out there?"

A low growl began to rise up from somewhere deep within the dog's body.

"Are those raccoons clawing through my compost again?" Ernie said, with a sigh. "Or maybe they're trying to get into the stable, huh?"

Jaeger growled.

Years ago, Ernie owned a few horses and had made a living renting them out to tourists to take on trail rides during the summer months. But since his wife had died, he'd gotten rid of all but a single horse – an old nag he'd named Sir Brian Hewlitt, after a knight he'd read about as a child – using the empty space in the stable to raise a few rabbits.

"I don't care what that Ranger Brock's got to say about preservin' wildlife," Ernie said, scowling. "If them raccoons can't stay away from my animals, I'm gonna set me some traps and shoot the damn things. Raccoons ain't no wildlife, they're just pests. Plain and simple."

The dog was up on all fours now, eyes fixed on the back door of the cabin.

Ernie got up then too, his aged body rising out of his chair a little at a time, until he was standing upright. "You want out, do you?"

Jaeger barked once and ran to the door. He reared up on his hind legs and desperately pawed at the doorknob.

"Hold on a minute," Ernie said. "Let me get that for ya." He turned the doorknob and pushed open the door.

Jaeger charged into the darkness, snarling and barking every step of the way.

"Go get 'em, boy!" Ernie cheered, then hurried over to the closet, where he kept all his coats and shoes. After slipping on his lumberjack jacket and stepping into a pair of winter boots, he pulled a hat over his head and searched the closet for a flashlight.

Meanwhile, there was noise outside, most likely coming from the stable. It was a pounding sound, as if the door was being knocked down by a fire brigade. Suddenly an awful screech pierced the night, like something was being torn apart.

"What the hell is going on out there?" Ernie shouted toward the open door. He scrambled over to the wall by the stove, where his Remington was locked securely in its rack.

Even more commotion outside now . . . like things inside the stable were being smashed and broken. The horse – Sir Brian Hewlitt – was neighing and stomping its hooves, as if trying to get out. On top of that was Jaeger's constant snarling and barking, as though the dog had someone or something pinned into a corner.

Ernie fumbled with his key chain, at first having a hard time finding the right key, then having little luck sliding that key into the padlock securing the shotgun. And while he struggled with the lock, a tremendous roar came from outside. It was so loud that Ernie could feel it in his bones. He'd never heard anything like it before, but if he had to guess, he'd say it came from something big, like a grizzly bear . . . a mean one, to boot.

Finally, the key slipped into the hole, and in a single motion, Ernie turned the key and popped open the lock. A second later, he was heading toward the open door with the loaded gun in his hands. But before he even reached the door, there was a sharp yelp, and Jaeger's barking – as well as all the other noises that had been coming from the stable – stopped abruptly.

"Who's there?" Ernie shouted into the darkness. He held the shotgun in his right hand, tucking the butt under his arm so he could keep the gun aimed while using his left hand to shine his flashlight into the forest.

There – movement among the trees.

As he adjusted the direction of the beam, he caught sight of a pair of wolves darting between two trees, one of them with a rabbit clenched in its maw.

"Damn wolves!" he cried, dropping the flashlight and squeezing off two rounds from his shotgun.

There were two brilliant flashes from the muzzle and, for an instant, the entire forest seemed ablaze with light. But despite the momentary illumination, there was no longer a sign of a wolf anywhere in the forest.

Ernie took a deep breath and picked up his flashlight. He shone the light, first at the forest, then slowly panned its beam toward the stable. The door had been bashed in and was hanging askew on just one of its hinges. In front, tufts of downy fur floated gently on the air like snowflakes.

"That's not a good sign," Ernie said.

He rushed over to the stable, slowing as he neared the front door in case one or more of the wolves were still inside. Then, standing to the side of the door, he shone the light inside.

All of the rabbit cages appeared to be intact, except for one. That cage had been ripped apart, and the rabbits that had been inside were gone. There was no mystery to that, since Ernie had seen a wolf running away with one of the rabbits in its mouth. But the question remained: What kind of wolf had the strength and ability to tear open a heavy steel cage as if it were made of Christmas wrap and ribbon?

He directed his light deeper into the stable and saw Sir Brian Hewlitt backed into a corner. The horse's body pressed against the far wall, still cowering from whatever it was that had been in the stable. And its eyes . . . its eyes were open wide in terror, looking like a pair of full moons in the darkness.

"It's okay, Sir Brian," Ernie said. "Everything's okay. It's gone now. . . ." Then, under his breath, "Whatever it was."

Obviously these were no ordinary wolves, if that's, in fact, what they were. But no matter how smart or strong they could be, Ernie took comfort in knowing that they wouldn't be able to outrun a round of buckshot. The thought reminded him that he'd taken shots at one of the wolves as it ran away. If he was lucky, he'd hit it and he'd find it lying somewhere in the snow, either dead or dying – he didn't care which.

He pumped another round into the chamber of his shotgun and headed toward the area of the forest where he'd last seen the wolves. As the beam from his flashlight swept over the snow, he noticed that the wolves had left behind plenty of tracks for him to follow.

And blood.

There were spatters and streaks of it all over the ground between the stable and the edge of the forest. But while Ernie should have been encouraged by the sight of all that blood, it left him feeling uneasy. There was just too much of it. If he'd hit one of the wolves, there would have been a few spatters, or maybe even a trail of blood leading into the forest. Instead, there were pools of it. And several angry red slashes seemed to be cut in the snow.

As he reached the line of trees at the edge of his yard, the bloodstains suddenly stopped and the snow leading into the forest was white and pure.

And that's when he kicked something with one of his boots, something soft, wet, and red.

Ernie shone the flashlight at his feet . . . and saw Jaeger lying there, dead.

What he'd first thought was a big red pool of blood in the snow was actually his trusted companion, torn up by half a dozen wolves or more, from the looks of it.

Ernie fell to his knees and placed a hand on his best friend's head. "Don't worry, boy," he sobbed. "I'll make those wolves pay."

Chapter 2

Noble opened up the textbook and began to read. "Okay . . . 1. Sketch a coordinate grid and choose any two points on the grid. Call these points *A* and *B*. Now, how is the line segment joining *A* and *B* different from the line that passes through *A* and *B*?"

Argus stared at the book for a while, then said, "What's a coordinate grid?"

Noble sighed. Argus had always had trouble with mathematics, but sometimes it seemed like he wasn't even trying. Still, Noble tried to answer his brother's questions as best he could. "A coordinate grid is a sort of diagram with horizontal and vertical lines on it that allow you to plot points on a plane."

"A plane? I thought we were studying math?"

"We are."

"Oh." Argus shook his head. "Why do I have to know this stuff, anyway?"

"Well, for one, coordinate grids are used by surveyors to plot out land and building sites." And then Noble was struck with an idea about how to catch Argus's interest. "I bet forest rangers use coordinate grids all the time."

"You think so?" Argus asked.

"We could ask the ranger."

Argus sighed. "I don't think I'm ever going to understand this stuff."

"Don't say things like that. Of course you'll get it," Noble said. "It's just a bit tricky, that's all."

Argus smiled at his brother. "Crossing Niagara Falls on a tightrope is *tricky*. Finding gold in the Yukon is *tricky*. Getting me to understand high school math is *impossible*."

Noble wasn't having any of it. "Nonsense," he said. "A lot of people have a hard time with math in high school, but they get it eventually . . . some of them even wind up being geniuses."

"Yeah, like who?"

"Albert Einstein, for one."

"Who?"

"Einstein," Noble said. "He came up with the Theory of Relativity – you know, *E* equals *MC* squared."

"What's that mean?"

Noble thought for a moment. "I don't know. All I know is, Einstein was a genius and he struggled with math, just like you."

"Actually," said Harlan over his shoulder, as he sat at the computer desk in the bedroom listening to Argus and Noble talk, "Einstein never struggled with math. What happened was, he got so bored with his schoolwork that he just stopped doing it. That's why he failed math, and that's why he got kicked out of school."

"You're not helping here, Harlan."

"Sorry."

The expression on Argus's face had become a strange mix of frustration, anger, and panic, as if his life were quickly spinning out of control. "I don't want to be a genius," he told Noble. "I just want to be a forest ranger like Ranger Brock, and a forest ranger doesn't have to know high school math."

"Maybe, maybe not," said Noble. "But a forest ranger does need to have a high school diploma, and you can't get one unless you pass math."

Argus's face suddenly brightened as his attention shifted from Noble to Harlan and the computer terminal on the desk in front of him. "Why don't you just hack into the school's computer and fix my mark, like you did before?" he said. "I don't need anything fancy, just enough to pass."

Harlan shook his head. "I can't do that anymore. The school has better protection against that sort of thing now, and they might even be able to figure out where the tampering came from. Besides, your math teacher, Mr. Surujpaul, knows you're struggling and he'd realize something was fishy if you suddenly had a passing grade."

"Especially when you haven't gotten over fifty on a single test this semester," Noble added.

Argus let out a long sigh. "Are you sure there isn't an easier way to get through this than studying?"

"Sorry, Argus," Noble said, "you're just going to have to do it on your own."

Argus shook his head in dismay, then cracked open his math textbook and began to read.

Just then the phone rang.

Ranger Brock answered, picking it up in the living room, just outside the boys' bedroom.

"Hello?" said Ranger Brock.

"Hi, Garrett," said the voice at the other end. "Konrad Martin here."

Konrad Martin was the sergeant in charge of the local detachment of the Royal Canadian Mounted Police. He worked closely with Garrett Brock – himself a peace officer – to enforce the laws to preserve the forests around Redstone, for both the wildlife as well as the citizens.

"Evening, Sergeant," Garrett said, then hesitated as he looked at his wristwatch. "To what do I owe the honor of a call at this late hour?"

"Ernie Ilson."

"The crazy trapper that lives halfway up the mountain?"

"That's him."

"I thought he died."

"No, that was his wife. He's still on the mountain, except he doesn't do much trapping anymore. Breeds rabbits instead, and does some logging work now and then."

"Okay, I know who he is," said the ranger. "What about him?"

"Well," the sergeant sighed. "He says he's just lost a few of his animals – a couple of rabbits and his dog, Jaeger." A pause. "Says they were killed by wolves."

Garrett said nothing for a moment. Then finally, "Wolves, you say."

At the mention of wolves, Garrett's wife, Phyllis, came into the room. She stood silently by her husband's side, her hands folded across her stomach and a look of grave concern on her face.

"I didn't say that," said the sergeant. "Ernie Ilson did."

"Wolves don't kill dogs," Garrett said. "And they sure don't break into cages and steal rabbits."

"Well, this one did," said the sergeant. "Ernie said he saw it running into the forest with one of his rabbits in its mouth."

Garrett had no response. This was bad news, as much for what had happened as for the timing of it. Redstone had just finished dealing with a story about killer wolves and a lost little girl who had to be rescued from a starving pack of them. If these were the same wolves, the people of Redstone still had a problem on their hands. Perhaps a bigger problem than even Ernie Ilson and the sergeant realized.

"Ernie's pretty upset," said the sergeant. "That dog was everything to him. . . ."

"Yeah, I bet."

"He's all fired up and wants to get a posse together to hunt down these wolves before anyone else loses an animal."

Garrett shook his head. "Guns are a bad idea."

"I told him that. Told him a lot of other things too, but nothing's getting through. Which sort of brings me to why I'm calling."

"You think I can convince him to put down his gun?" Garrett said, unable to keep his doubt from affecting his voice.

The phone was silent a moment and the ranger could picture the sergeant shrugging his shoulders. "It's worth a try," the sergeant said. "Besides, you're going to want to come by and see the dog's body and the rabbit cages . . . so it might as well be now, as opposed to later."

"Can you keep him from shooting anybody til I get there?"

"I'll handcuff him to a rail if I have to."

"All right, then," Garrett said. "I'm on my way."

Noble, Argus, and Harlan were all sitting in silence as the ranger hung up the phone. They'd been listening to his side of the conversation and had been able to figure out what Sergeant Martin had been saying. Something had gotten into Ernie Ilson's rabbit pens, stealing two of the rabbits and killing his dog. Mr. Ilson and the sergeant were blaming it on wolves, but the pack wasn't so sure.

"Are you thinking what I'm thinking?" Noble asked his brothers.

"I didn't think the change would come over the wolf so quickly," Argus said. "It's barely had enough time to heal from its wounds."

Harlan spun around in his chair, putting his back to the computer screen. "Maybe it isn't the new werewolf."

"No?" Argus said. "What else could it be?"

Harlan shrugged. "It *could* be the other wolves. They were ready to eat a little girl. If they were that hungry, what would stop them from getting at a couple of rabbits – certainly not a dog."

The brothers seemed unconvinced.

"Or . . . how about a bear?" Harlan continued. "A bear would be strong enough to do it."

Noble shook his head. "Except just about every bear on the mountain is hibernating now."

"Oh, yeah." Harlan's eyes dropped to the floor a moment, then rose up again, as eager as ever. "Or maybe it was a big cat. You know, a lynx or a bobcat, maybe even a mountain lion."

That was a possibility, but a cat, even a big one, would have had trouble pushing in a door and ripping open a cage. That required size and strength, and a pair of hands that could grip and pull against each other. The only thing that could do all that was . . .

"Why don't we go see for ourselves." The three brothers turned to find their sister, Tora, standing in the bedroom doorway. "I know where Ernie Ilson lives," she said. "It wouldn't take us long to get there through the forest."

"Great idea," said Harlan. "Let's go!"

"Yeah," said Argus, rising to his feet. "We could probably get there even before the ranger does."

But Noble was hesitant. "I don't know if that's such a good idea."

"Why not?" Tora said, stepping into their bedroom and closing the door behind her.

"Mr. Ilson says he's lost three animals to wolves; he's got his shotgun out and he's shooting to kill. Maybe it's not the best time to be running through the forest in our wolfen form," Noble said.

"That's *if* they even were wolves," Harlan reminded his brother.

"Whether they were wolves or not is not the point," Noble said. "Mr. Ilson *believes* they were wolves and he'll be shooting first and asking questions later." Noble let out a sigh. "It's not exactly a good time to be a wolf right now."

"It hasn't been for a while," Tora muttered, under her breath.

She had a point. The last few weeks had been rough on the pack, with Maria Abruzzo claiming that wolves had taken her younger sister into the forest. The pack had rescued the lost girl, and people in town had pretty much put that episode behind them. Even Maria herself had since accepted the pack for who and what they were. Still, people's fear of wolves ran deep and this latest episode threatened to destroy all the goodwill the pack had fought so hard to win.

"I'm just saying that if people are out gunning for wolves – any wolves – it might be an idea to wait here and see what happens."

"Have you lost your nerve?" Argus asked.

Noble looked at his brother, thinking about what he'd said. *Have I lost my nerve?* he wondered. *Did getting poisoned with silver take some of my edge away?* It was possible. After all, he'd nearly died from it, and death was the sort of thing that made people appreciate life a whole lot more. No, he wasn't afraid of what was out there in the forest, just wary of it.

"I'm simply being cautious," Noble said, at last. "Aside from angry people with guns, we don't know what else might be out there."

That seemed to bring the others around to Noble's way of thinking. While they all had a feeling there might be a new werewolf in the forest, none of them had any idea of what it might look like. *How big might it be? How strong? How wild?*

Argus, however, still needed convincing. "Look," he said. "The ranger and Sergeant Martin will deal with Ernie Ilson. He won't be shooting at any more wolves for a while, at least not tonight. That leaves the thing in the forest. Who knows what it's doing, or what its plans are? For all we know, it could be killing someone else's pet as we speak."

A moment of dead silence.

Then Harlan said, "I could track it." He had been suffering from a cold and a stuffed-up nose, but he'd gotten over it weeks ago. His sense of smell was as good as ever.

"And we don't have to confront it," Tora suggested. "All we have to do is find out what it is. That would be a big help to the ranger, wouldn't it?"

Noble looked at his siblings in turn, trying to come up with a reason to disagree with them.

But he couldn't.

"All right," he said, at last. "We'll go and check things out in the forest around Mr. Ilson's place. But whatever we find, we're only going to observe and report back to the ranger. It'll be up to him and the sergeant to decide what's best to do. Agreed?"

"All right," said Harlan.

Tora nodded. "Sounds like a plan."

Argus took a deep breath and sighed. It was in his nature to want to take a more active approach to solving these kinds of problems – by, say, killing whatever it was that was causing the problem – but even he had to admit that this situation required that they proceed with caution. "Agreed," he said.

"Good," Noble said. "Let's go."

As the pack rose to their feet, the bedroom door opened.

"Where are you all going?" Phyllis stood in the doorway, her fists on her hips.

Noble thought about lying to her, but he couldn't bring himself to do it. "We thought we'd go by Mr. Ilson's place. Maybe we can help the ranger figure out what happened."

Phyllis pondered that a moment. "He thought you might have overheard that phone call," she said. "He doesn't want you going near there."

"We aren't planning on getting too close," Noble said. That wasn't exactly a lie. They weren't *planning* on getting close, but who knew, the situation might change once they got there.

"As long as you keep your distance."

"We will," said Noble.

The others nodded in agreement as they filed out of the bedroom.

"All right, then," Phyllis said. "The last thing we need right now is for any of you to get into trouble."

The only answer was the back door slamming shut.

Chapter 3

Garrett Brock knocked on the door of Ernie Ilson's cabin. The lights were on inside, and he could hear Ernie and Sergeant Martin talking. After the knock, the conversation inside ended and someone came to open the door.

Ernie was standing there with glassy eyes, tear-streaked cheeks, and a look on his face like he'd just lost his best friend.

"Hello, Ernie," the ranger said.

"Hey," the old-timer said, acknowledging the ranger with a wave of his hand.

Garrett smelled alcohol on the man's breath and, from the look of him, it was obvious he'd had a drink or two. The ranger couldn't fault him for that. He and that dog had been inseparable . . . til now.

Ernie turned and headed back to his chair. Sergeant Martin was on the couch facing the chair, a nice fire burning in the stove. The cabin was a bit cramped, but it suited Ernie's needs. With his rabbits, a small vegetable garden in the summer, and a good-sized generator, he didn't have to venture into Redstone but a couple of times a year for supplies.

"Thanks for coming," said the sergeant.

Garrett acknowledged his friend with a nod and then pulled up a stool to sit down.

"Don't get too comfortable," Ernie said, walking past his chair and picking up his jacket and shotgun. "You've come to see what's outside, so we might as well get to it so you and the sergeant can be on your way."

The ranger and the sergeant got up and followed Ernie outside. All three of the men carried flashlights and were easily able to illuminate the tracks left behind in the snow. There were several sets of wolf tracks, but also other tracks that were larger, both in the size of the paw prints and the distance between them. The prints looked as if they *could* belong to a wolf, but the stride suggested the wolf was huge.

"Wow," said the sergeant. "Those are the biggest I've seen for a wolf." He turned to Ernie. "You sure it wasn't a bear?"

The question angered the old man. "I've lived in these woods more than fifty years. Think I don't know the difference between a bear and a wolf?"

"Just asking."

Garrett nodded. The sergeant had been right to ask the question, since the tracks had many similarities with those of a bear. And whatever had made the tracks had been walking on two feet rather than four. Bears walked like that from time to time, but so did werewolves. . . .

While the sergeant's instincts were right, Garrett wasn't about to help the man come to the correct conclusion. This was a problem that he and the pack had to handle on their own. The less the sergeant knew about the truth, the better.

"Wolf tracks," the ranger said at last, with an exaggerated nod. "It's a big one, for sure."

"See!" said Ernie. "I told ya."

Sergeant Martin looked over at Garrett with slightly narrowed eyes. He'd worked out of the Redstone detachment for some fifteen years and he'd spent enough time in the forest to know what different animal tracks looked like. Of course he would bow to the ranger's expertise, but that didn't mean he couldn't still be suspicious. "You sure about that?" he asked.

"Trust me" was all the ranger said.

The sergeant took a moment to consider that. "All right then, it was a wolf. Let's go see the rabbit pens."

Ernie led them to the stable. The door was still hanging by one hinge and had to be carefully pushed back to allow the three men inside. "There, look at that!"

The three of them shone their lights on the cages. The remaining rabbits were all huddled in tight packs in the corners of their cages, as far away from the door as possible. There was a jittery nervousness about the animals, who jumped at every noise and movement around them. But the most disturbing thing of all was the middle cage. It had been ripped open, like someone might tear into a plastic bag to get at the candies. The metal was stretched, torn, and mangled, as if the heavy-gauge steel cage had been made of twist ties.

Ranger Brock noticed movement in the background and shone his light deeper into the stable. Ernie's horse was there, trying to hide in the depths of the shadows instead of approaching them. That was strange, since Sir Brian Hewlitt was a gentle animal, one of the most friendly and curious horses the ranger had ever seen. Obviously something had spooked it – big time.

"You're saying wolves did this?" the sergeant asked, at last.

"Hard to believe, I know," said Ernie, "but I saw two of them leaving. And they had one of my rabbits with them."

The sergeant looked to Garrett for confirmation or denial. It didn't seem possible that wolves could grab the cage firmly enough to pry it open like that, but strange things seemed to happen around Redstone all the time.

"There was a big wolf," the ranger said. "Very big. And if something that big gets hungry enough, who knows what it's capable of doing."

"If you say it was a wolf, then it was a wolf." The sergeant said the words, but his tone hinted that he didn't totally believe it.

Ernie swept his light across the backyard and focused his beam on something on the ground by the edge of the forest. "And then there's Jaeger." He sniffed back a tear. "You two have a look. I don't want to see it again tonight."

Without a word, the ranger and the sergeant headed across the yard. As they approached, they could smell the animal's blood in the air.

"It's the dog," the sergeant said, shining his light on the body.

Garrett put his flashlight beam onto the dog's head, then moved it slowly down the body. The animal's fur was soaked with blood and much of it had already dried black. There were four parallel slashes down the neck, each one about four inches long and spaced an inch apart. And chunks of flesh had been torn from the animal's body.

"You still sure a wolf did this?"

Garrett didn't know what to say. He couldn't outright lie, but neither could he tell the truth. "Something *like* a wolf, maybe," he said.

"*Like* a wolf?" A pause. "Do I need to know more about this?"

It was a curious question. The ranger had never told the sergeant the pack's secret, and the sergeant had never asked. But now, it was obvious that the man had his suspicions, possibly like other people in Redstone.

Garrett shook his head. "No. I don't think you do."

Sergeant Martin let out a sigh. "All right, but what are we going to do now? If other people start losing animals, they'll expect something to be done about it."

"You take care of the people in town and leave the forest to me."

The sergeant nodded.

Just then their attention was caught by Ernie's flashlight as he panned his beam past them and into the forest.

"What are you doing?" the sergeant asked.

"They're still out there," he answered. "And I'm going to find 'em. And when I find 'em, I'm going to kill 'em."

The two men walked over to where Ernie stood, his shotgun raised waist high and his finger clearly on the trigger.

"Nobody's going to be killing anything," said the sergeant, putting a hand on the barrel of Ernie's gun and guiding it safely toward the ground.

"But they're in the forest. I *know* it," Ernie said.

"They might be," said the ranger. "But all you're going to do is get yourself killed, wandering through the forest in the middle of the night."

"You saying you're going to let 'em get away with it?"

The ranger shook his head. "No one's getting away with anything. But you know as well as anyone that if you live up on the mountain with wild animals, every once in a while things like this are going to happen." There'd been many times the ranger had been called into Redstone to wrangle a mountain lion or bear that had wandered down main street, or was napping in the school yard behind Redstone Elementary.

"But they killed Jaeger!" Ernie shouted. He stood there

a moment – his body shaking uncontrollably – until he suddenly broke down and cried.

Garrett placed a hand on the man's shoulder. "We know how much he meant to you and we're sorry. But killing a wolf won't make things right. We've got to track the animals, trap them, and relocate them – maybe north, maybe east. It's going to take some time, so you'll just have to be patient."

They guided Ernie back to the cabin.

"And, in the meantime," said the sergeant, "no hunting wolves."

"Yeah, yeah, yeah."

"That's not good enough. . . . You have to promise me that you won't be heading out into the forest."

"All right, I promise."

Satisfied that the old man was calm enough to be left alone, Garrett and the sergeant prepared to leave. But before they did, Garrett asked Ernie, "Would you like me to take Jaeger's body away for you?"

Ernie sniffed and shook his head. "No, I'll give him a proper burial in the morning. I should be okay to deal with it by then."

Garrett said, "Take care. I'll be in touch." He watched Ernie step into the cabin and close the door behind him, then he followed the sergeant around the house to where his 4 x 4 was parked.

"Do you think he'll stay out of the forest?" Garrett asked the sergeant.

"He gave me his word."

"Yeah, but do you think it means anything?"

The sergeant shrugged. "Who knows?"

After the sergeant and the ranger drove away, Ernie spent some time in front of the stove. He was tired, but there was no way he'd be getting any sleep. His mind was too bent on revenge. Those beasts in the forest had killed his best friend and at least one of them was going to pay for it. If he could get more, then even better.

But he'd promised the sergeant he'd stay out of the forest, so hunting the animals down tonight was out of the question. If nothing else, Ernie Ilson was a man of his word.

But what if? . . .

What if he just waited for the beasts to return? What if he sat outside on the back porch until one of them returned for Jaeger's body? If the animals came to him, it wouldn't be hunting, would it? All he'd be doing is protecting his property.

That was it. That's what he'd do.

And so he went back to the closet for more clothes and put on enough layers so he could wait outside for hours without getting cold.

He was about to head for the back door when he stopped and turned. Reaching down, he picked up the bottle of whiskey he'd been drinking and took that with him . . . to help with the cold.

Finally outside, he eased back into one of the Muskoka

chairs he kept on the porch behind the cabin, took a swig from the bottle, and lay the shotgun across his lap.

"Here, wolf!" he whispered, under his breath. "I got something for ya and it ain't goin' to hurt a bit."

With that, a slight smile crept across Ernie's face.

It wouldn't hurt because dead wolves feel no pain.

The pack ran carefully through the forest, wary of what they might find between the trees. They were heedful not to overtake Harlan as he followed the scent of wolves. Harlan was crouched down low, sniffing as he went. Every once in a while, he would stop, raise his head, and look around, then it was nose to the ground and forward, step-by-step.

All at once, Harlan stopped.

The rest of the pack stopped behind him, waiting in silence and wondering what he had found.

Harlan looked ahead a moment, then leaped forward, bounding down the trail several meters before coming to a halt over a bloody patch in the snow.

The others came up behind him, and it didn't take long before they were all standing around the remains of one of Ernie Ilson's rabbits.

Harlan was the first to change his shape so he could speak. "It was wolves," he said. "The same ones that were stalking Angelina Abruzzo."

Noble looked at the dark spot on the snow. The rabbit had been ravaged by several wolves at once, judging by the state of what was left.

"They were hungry," said Argus, explaining the wolves' frenzy. "They did what they had to do to survive."

But Noble couldn't help feel there was something more to this. Sure, the winter had been a cold one and sources of food were hard to come by, but these wolves were expert hunters and should have been able to find food in the forest, especially now that they were being led by a werewolf. But even if the wolves were simply desperate for food, the people of Redstone wouldn't see it that way. They would look upon this as trespassing, or worse, an outright attack against a man's home and property.

And that man wouldn't take it lightly. He would fight back and get others to help him. Man versus nature. And neither side would win.

Noble let out a sigh.

Harlan suddenly rose up, sniffing the air as a light breeze blew up the mountain.

"What is it?" Noble asked.

"Something bigger," Harlan said, gesturing down the mountain.

Noble looked below and recognized the outline of Mr. Ilson's cabin through the trees. The place was dark and Noble figured the old man had probably gone to bed.

Suddenly Harlan was on the move, heading down the mountain. He was making a beeline for the house, tracking a scent along the way. Finally, he stopped at the edge of the forest, about ten meters from Mr. Ilson's back porch.

Noble and the others came up behind Harlan, content to look over his shoulder at what lay on the ground at his feet.

Mr. Ilson's dog.

There were four bloody slashes across its throat, and it had been partially eaten. The werewolf had killed it with a single swipe of its massive talons. In just a few short days, the wild wolf pack's alpha male had recovered from its fight with Argus, transformed itself into a werewolf, and became an efficient and deadly killer.

What's happened? Noble thought. *What have we done?*

Meanwhile, Argus took his full werewolf shape and placed one of his talons on each of the slashes on the dog's throat to measure what size of hand had caused the wound. The werewolf was at least as big as Argus, perhaps even bigger. A look of grave concern crossed Argus's face. If Argus had had a hard enough time defeating the wolf while he was in his werewolf form, what kind of fight would it be if they were both werewolves?

"Your brother, Argus," Noble said. "Or perhaps your son."

"What?" asked Argus.

"You created him."

"We had no choice," Tora said, jumping in to defend Argus and her decision to let him fight the wild pack's alpha male. "Argus had to fight the wolf. If he didn't, Angelina would have been eaten alive."

Noble hated to second-guess his sister. From all accounts, she had done an excellent job leading the pack in his absence, so it wasn't right for him to judge her actions. Still, while they'd saved Angelina Abruzzo, they had also created a *monster*, and now not just a little girl, but everyone in Redstone was in danger.

"Was there no other way?" Noble asked.

"It was the right thing to do,"Tora said, a trace of despair in her voice, even through the rough rasp of her half-human form.

Noble was about to apologize to his sister when another voice called out.

"Who's out there?" it said. "I knew you'd be back."

And, a moment later –

BOOM!

A gunshot split apart the silence of the forest.

A tree to the left of them exploded into splinters, and Mr. Ilson was running toward them, his gun leveled at the waist.

Without a moment's hesitation, all four pack members lunged into the forest. Shots rang out behind them. Snow and tree branches began to fall around them.

They never looked back, but kept on running for a long, long time.

Chapter 4

It may have been the small hours of the morning, but the Brock clan was huddled around the kitchen table, sipping warm milk and eating freshly made cookies.

"The rabbit was far from the house," said Harlan. "Fifty meters, maybe more."

"And it had been chewed up," Argus added. "There was nothing left but pieces of fur and bits of bone."

"Then there was the dog," said Tora.

"I saw it, thanks," said the ranger, lifting his hand in order to be spared the gory details.

"Yeah, we were looking at it. . . ," said Noble.

But Harlan picked up where his brother left off. "And that's when Mr. Ilson shot at us."

"What!" said the ranger, nearly jumping out of his seat.

"He took a shot at you?" Phyllis said, also rising up at the table.

"We were in our wolfen form," explained Noble. "He was either guarding the dog, or waiting for the wolves to come back."

Argus shrugged. "And when he saw us, he took a shot."

The ranger took a deep breath. "Was anyone hurt?"

They all shook their heads.

"But there's one less tree out behind his house," said Argus.

The pack laughed at that, but the ranger and Phyllis didn't find it funny. "You four have got to be more careful," he said. "I don't want you going anywhere near that place, not as wolves . . . not even as humans. Understood?"

The pack hesitated a moment, but all of them nodded in agreement. "Yes, ranger," Noble said, speaking for the group.

Ranger Brock said nothing for few moments, giving himself the chance to calm down. Finally he said, "Now, where were we?"

Noble leaned forward and rested his elbows on the table. "We were talking about the dog. Obviously, it wasn't killed by any wolf. Not one, not two. Not even a whole pack."

"Well," the ranger sighed. "That's the official story, as far as I'm concerned right now. It's what Ernie Ilson thinks, and it's what I told Sergeant Martin."

"He believes you?" Argus asked.

"I don't know. It doesn't really matter. I told him it was wolves and he trusts me enough to put that into the occurrence police report."

Just then the phone rang. Phyllis, who was sitting closest to it, got up from her chair to answer it.

The ranger and the pack all fell silent, eager to know who would be calling at this time of night.

"Hello?"

A pause.

"Oh, hi, Erin, how are you?" Phyllis said, chatting quietly in the corner, away from the rest of them.

As she talked, Noble picked up the conversation where they'd left off. "So if the sergeant doesn't really think it's wolves, what's the rest of the town going to think?"

"We can't worry about that now," the ranger said. "There's a wild wolf man running loose in the forest and the first thing we've got to do is make sure everyone is safe."

Tora snickered.

Argus looked at her. "What's so funny?"

"He called it a *wolf man*."

Everyone looked to the ranger for a response.

"That's right, a wolf man," he said. "Sure it's a werewolf, like you four are, but it's also a totally wild animal. It hasn't been part man for more than a few days and it doesn't know right from wrong. That *thing* out there is a wolf that's suddenly become a man. Just last week, it was hunting down a little girl to feed itself and its pack. This week, it's still that same animal, only now it's bigger, stronger, and smarter. It's capable of doing just about anything, and there's nothing in its head or its heart that will stop it from killing – either for food or to defend itself. Worst of all, we're the only people trying to stop it . . ." (the ranger gestured to everyone in the kitchen, then pointed in the direction of Redstone) ". . . while there are hundreds of people in town that just want to shoot it dead."

"But they won't be able to kill it without silver bullets," offered Noble. They all knew a werewolf could be hurt by a regular gunshot, but not killed.

"I wouldn't be surprised if some people are brushing a bit of silver paint on their bullets, or making shotgun shells packed with bits of silver, just to be safe," the ranger added.

No one said a word. Even Phyllis paused in the middle of her phone conversation.

"What if. . . ," Tora said, breaking the silence. "What if what happened at Mr. Ilson's was an isolated incident? What if the . . . the wolf man has led his pack away from the area, now that they've had a meal?"

Argus shook his head. "That's not going to happen. The pack was starving, might still be starving. If they've found an easy source of food, they're not going anywhere until the spring, and even then they might not leave."

"So what are we going to do?" Harlan asked.

The ranger shrugged. "There's not a lot we *can* do right now. I'm hoping we might be able to communicate with the wolf man somehow, or maybe you four can talk to it." The tone in his voice said that even he felt these were longshots.

"We're not so good at howling," said Noble.

"We can do it," Argus said. "But we really don't know what we're saying."

"If anything," Harlan added.

"It was just a thought." The ranger shrugged. "In the meantime, I'll be setting a few traps. Maybe there's a chance we can catch it and take it farther north."

"Hey, take it from me," Tora said, with a smile. "Werewolves *can* be trapped."

"That's right," said Noble. "Maybe even the wolf man can be trapped."

At that moment Phyllis hung up the phone. The look on her face said that she had some news to share.

"That was Erin McMillan, who's on the fundraising committee of the 'Friends of the Redstone Library.' You remember her, Garrett – big blonde hair, green eyes, a real chatterbox."

"Sounds familiar," the ranger said.

"She called to say that Ernie Ilson has been on the phone with everyone in Redstone, demanding a town meeting to talk about what's got to be done about . . . *the plague*."

"Plague?" said Harlan.

"What plague?" added the ranger.

"The plague. . . ," Phyllis said, moving her head slightly from side to side, "of killer wolves infecting Redstone."

"You must be kidding," muttered the ranger.

"I'm afraid not," Phyllis said.

"What do you think I should do?" he asked.

Everyone turned to Phyllis.

"I think," she said, "you should go to that meeting."

"Yeah," the ranger replied. "I think you're right."

Chapter 5

Life at Redstone Secondary School had slowly settled into a pleasant routine for the pack. After Argus and the others had found Angelina Abruzzo in the woods and were instrumental in getting her the medical attention that saved her life, a feeling of acceptance settled upon the students. And with Jake McKinnon, the school bully, serving time in a closed-custody facility up near Smithers, no one was calling Harlan "dogface" anymore. Best of all, Tora and Maria Abruzzo were getting along famously. They were meeting regularly in the halls for chats, talking on MSN at night, and even eating lunch together in the school cafeteria.

That's why the attack on Mr. Ilson's animals was so disheartening to the pack. After fifteen long years of being on the outside looking in, here they were *on the inside*, so accepted in the school that no one looked twice at them anymore, or called them names. If news got out that it wasn't just wolves terrorizing the town, but a werewolf . . . a *wolf man*, then everyone would be afraid of them again and it wouldn't be safe to go to school anymore.

But that hadn't happened, yet. So far, the attack had been an isolated incident, and with the ranger and the sergeant working to prevent further losses of property or life, chances were good the pack could continue to enjoy things for at least a few more days.

During lunch period, Tora met Maria in the far corner of the cafeteria. She loved sitting with Maria, talking about everything from their favorite reality TV shows to the cutest guys in the school. It was a great break from eating lunch with her brothers – which she'd done just about every day she'd been at the school – and it made her feel like she belonged.

"Hi, Tora," Maria said one day, sliding over to make room.

Tora sat down next to her. "Hey, Maria," she said. "Do you have anything to trade?"

Being Italian, Maria Abruzzo had things in her lunch that Tora had never eaten before – sometimes Boccaccini cheese, which was a little bit salty and had the texture of bubble gum; sometimes salami, prosciutto, or capicolo. Tora had asked Phyllis if she could buy some of these delicious meats, but Phyllis and Mrs. Abruzzo didn't shop at the same grocery store, so trading parts of her lunch became a treat for Tora.

"Reggiano cheese," Maria said, handing a chunk to Tora, who popped it in her mouth. It was tart and tangy and made her mouth feel alive.

"Wow!" Tora said.

"You like that?"

"Yes, it's really good."

"My mother got it in Prince George," Maria said. "She buys a lot of food there whenever she goes . . . meats and cheeses especially. She says, 'If there was an Italian grocery store in Redstone, that would make it the perfect place to live.' "

Tora laughed. There were a lot of things she'd like to see in Redstone – like a bowling alley, or a big indoor mall – but maybe it could use an Italian grocer too.

Just then three of Maria's friends came into the cafeteria and walked past the table where Maria and Tora were sitting.

"Hey, guys!" she said, waving her hand. "I'm over here."

The three girls turned around, spotted Maria, and each gave a nod of their head. "Oh, we saw you," said Gabriela Santos, one of Maria's closest friends. "We need to study for a math test this afternoon." Then she turned and led the others to a table two rows away.

"That's strange," Maria said. "We always sit together at lunch."

Tora watched the girls take their seats. They began to eat their lunches, but only one had a textbook out on the table.

"They don't like me," Tora said.

"Nonsense," Maria replied. "They're my friends and you're my friend . . . that makes all of you my friends." She shrugged. "They need to study, that's all."

Tora wasn't convinced.

"Do you want another piece of cheese?" Maria said.

Tora looked into her lunch bag and saw that she had a ham sandwich on white bread, an apple, a granola bar, and a box of apricot-passion-fruit juice. "I'm afraid I don't have anything good to trade."

Maria shrugged. "Don't worry about it. My mother has twenty more pounds of this stuff at home."

Second Period. Math.

Argus lingered at his locker as long as he could, but when the hallway emptied and everyone was in class, there was no putting it off any longer.

He hated everything about math class – the color of the textbook, the row he sat in, the students around him, the stupid charts on the walls, the sound of chalk against the blackboard, the way the sun shone through the windows, the pattern of tile on the floor, Daniel Colp – the smartest guy in the class – the teacher, Mr. Surujpaul, the way he wore the same jacket and pants to school every day, the way he combed his hair, the stupid jokes he made (Q: What do you get if you divide the circumference of a jack-o'-lantern by its diameter? A: Pumpkin pi!), the pencil stub he had to use, the noise the sharpener made, the three minutes it took to take attendance and the other fifty-two minutes until the class was over. . . .

Argus hated math because he didn't get it. It wasn't that he didn't understand a few concepts here and there, he didn't get *any* of it. Perhaps it was the way Mr. Surujpaul explained things, or maybe his head wasn't wired for numbers. Whatever the reason, the moment class started, he immediately tuned out and, the next thing he knew, Mr. Surujpaul would ask him a question.

Like now.

". . . which gives us a factor of what . . . Argus Brock?"

"Huh?" Argus said, turning toward Mr. Surujpaul.

"Surely you've been following."

"Yes."

"Good. Then, what's the answer?"

Argus's mind had been off in the forest, running through the trees and hunting prey. He stared blankly at Mr. Surujpaul's green plaid jacket, his mouth open and sweat forming on his brow.

"I didn't hear you," Mr. Surujpaul said.

"I . . . uh."

A slight laugh began to circulate through the classroom. Argus could feel his face turning red.

"Did you do your homework last night?" Mr. Surujpaul said.

He had copied Harlan's answers into his book, but he hadn't really done any work.

"Yes," he said, at last.

"Let me see."

Argus turned his notebook around to let the teacher inspect it. All of the work was there, neatly copied from

Harlan's detailed notes. Argus had even copied every correction Harlan had made so it looked as if Argus had actually struggled to figure everything out.

Mr. Surujpaul looked at him. "So you did your homework, you just weren't paying attention?"

"That's right," he said.

"So what's more interesting than math?"

Argus glanced over at the windows.

"I see," the teacher said. "Next time, try to keep your mind in here with the rest of us."

"I will."

"Daniel," he said, knowing that Daniel Colp – Redstone Secondary's only Bushlen-Mowatt Teen Scholarship winner – would have the answer on the tip of his tongue.

"Forty-two," Daniel said, without hesitation.

"Right." And with that, Mr. Surujpaul strolled up the aisle, away from Argus's desk.

Argus watched the man take a few steps, then thought about the redwood forests in the fall – the smell of the earth and the color of the sunlight as it punched its way through the trees. And before he knew it, the bell rang, ending the day's torture session. Argus was one of the first to his feet and the first out the door.

"Don't forget the questions on page 112 for tomorrow," Mr. Surujpaul said, but by then Argus was halfway to his locker.

Just before last period that day, Argus saw a notice pinned up on the bulletin board outside Coach Quinn's phys ed office:

THE REDSTONE WARRIORS
CROSS-COUNTRY RUNNING TEAM
WILL BE HOLDING TRYOUTS
AFTER SCHOOL WEDNESDAY
IN THE GYM

He read it several times, thinking that cross-country running might be something he'd be good at.

"Hey, Argus," said Noble, appearing by Argus's side. "What's going on?"

Argus gestured at the notice. "Coach Quinn just put that up. What do you think?"

Noble took a moment to read the notice. "Forget about it," he said.

"Why?"

"You know that the ranger has told us many times he doesn't want us doing that sort of stuff. . . ," Noble looked left and right to see if anyone was listening, "because of who and what we are."

Argus kissed his teeth. "That was for *football.* He didn't want me joining the team because he was afraid the physical contact would, you know . . . get me angry and bring on the change. He was afraid I might hurt somebody. This," he said, tapping a finger against the notice, "this is just running. We go running all the time."

Noble was unconvinced. "You *will* ask him first," he said. "Get his permission."

"Yeah, of course," Argus answered, dismissing Noble's concerns with a wave of his hand. "The ranger has to let me run. I mean, what could possibly go wrong?"

Chapter 6

A half hour after dinner, Phyllis poked her head into the boys' room and said, "We're leaving now, if you want to come with us."

"I'll be right there," said Noble.

Ranger Brock was going into Redstone to speak to people angry that Ernie Ilson's rabbits and dog had been killed by a wolf. They wanted revenge for the deaths – they wanted the blood of the wolf and its pack splashed all over the forest floor. They wanted to know, at the very least, that the government – meaning Ranger Brock and British Columbia's Ministry of the Environment, Sergeant Martin and the RCMP, Mayor Magill and the city of Redstone – had a response to this threat.

Since the ranger couldn't promise the wolf would be killed, or the city would be safe, Noble wouldn't dare miss what was sure to be a very interesting meeting, so he'd finished all of his homework before supper.

"Me, too," said Argus, putting on his shoes.

Noble looked at his bigger brother with suspicion. "What about your math homework?" he asked. Argus hadn't cracked a book.

"We didn't get any homework," he answered.

Harlan stopped putting on his jacket. "We did too," he said. "All the questions on page 112."

Argus shrugged. "I didn't hear Mr. Surujpaul assign anything."

Harlan was having trouble believing that. Although each member of the pack had math at a different time, they were all taking the same course. "Are you sure you didn't just *not hear* the assignment?" he asked.

Argus shook his head. "Nope."

Tora appeared in the doorway. "What's going on?"

Harlan tilted his head in Argus's direction. "He says he didn't get any homework from Mr. Surujpaul."

"Uh-uh," said Tora. "I was just talking to Maria Abruzzo and she's got math homework tonight."

Argus gave a little sneer. "What does Maria Abruzzo know?"

Tora folded her arms across her chest. "Well, for one, she happens to be in your class."

"Really?"

"Yes. She even sits next to you."

"Oh."

"Time to go," Phyllis called from the hallway. "The ranger doesn't want to be late."

Noble, Tora, and Harlan all looked at Argus. "If Mr. Surujpaul gave us homework, I'll get it from someone else in the morning," he said, leaving the room.

"That stuff was hard," Harlan said, when Argus was gone. "Even for me."

"Maybe we should tell the ranger or Phyllis about Argus," said Tora. "Or at least try to help him if he's struggling."

"I've already tried that," said Harlan. "I don't think he wants our help."

"Harlan's right," said Noble. "We'll help Argus if he asks, but if he's going to fail, he'll do that all on his own."

The largest meeting room in the Redstone Community Center, the R.H. Gray Memorial Hall, was named after Robert Hampton Gray, the last Canadian to win a Victoria Cross in World War II.

But the history and sanctity of the room had little to do with what was going on in the hall on this night. It was crammed with Redstone citizens, and the din of voices could be heard outside, all the way to the parking lot. A slight pall of tobacco smoke hung in the air as several of Redstone's old-timers ignored the town's no-smoking bylaw, lighting up their pipes, cigarettes, and cigars.

"The natives are restless," said Ranger Brock, as he got out of the car.

"Ernie Ilson must have called all of his friends," Phyllis said.

"No," the ranger said, laughing under his breath. "Ernie doesn't have any friends. He must have called his enemies, or maybe everyone he owes money to."

Phyllis came around the front of the car and put a hand on the ranger's shoulder. "It won't do you any good to go in there angry."

Ranger Brock nodded and took a deep, deep breath.

"Do you know what you're going to tell them?" she asked.

"Not really. We're doing a couple of things, but there's nothing you'd really call a plan. I'm just hoping Konrad comes up with something."

"I'm sure it'll all work out," Phyllis said, running a hand up and down the ranger's back.

"Yeah, everything always works out in the end," he said. "It's the middle, where everything goes wrong, that's got me worried."

Phyllis smiled, remaining by the ranger's side all the way into the building.

The pack followed.

As he entered the room, the ranger was struck by the voices. A lot of them were talking at once, and he felt that they all were angry, some even wanting blood. When the people noticed him, the noise in the hall quieted to a low murmur.

Garrett left Phyllis and the pack to find seats for themselves at the back of the room, then he walked up a side aisle to the front. Sergeant Martin was already standing by the podium, and next to him was Mayor Magill, who also owned the only dry cleaners and movie rental in town. Garrett shook hands with the mayor, then the sergeant, and took a seat.

"All right, then," said the mayor. "Now that everybody's here, we can begin."

There was one last shifting of seats, then the room slowly grew silent.

The mayor waited a moment, then began. "As you know by now, Ernie Ilson was visited by some wolves last night."

"Wasn't just a visit," someone said, from the middle of the room. "It was a *raid*. A killing raid."

A clamor of voices erupted. When things calmed down, the mayor resumed his address. "Call it what you want, at this point it's an isolated incident."

"I've lost one of my cats," said Margaret Maynard, a sixty-year-old single woman who lived in a cabin on the edge of town.

"My dog's gone too!" said a man at the back.

"There's half a horse lying in my front yard and there's no sign of the rest of it anywhere," added Yvonne Nagleson, who ran a riding stable outside of Alexis Creek.

Garrett didn't like what he was hearing. There was a wild werewolf in the forest and it was acting like a killing machine, leaving a lot of angry people in its wake.

Suddenly a man stood up and pointed a finger at Ranger Brock. "This is all your fault, you know!" he said.

Garrett recognized him as Fatias Boyage, owner of the Crosscut and Curl Hair Salon in downtown Redstone.

"My fault?" Garrett said, placing an open hand against his chest as he rose from his chair.

"That's right," Fatias insisted, turning to include the people around him. "Our wolf troubles all started with that Doctor Monk. He wanted to take a wolf out of the forest and you wouldn't let him. If he'd taken that wolf away, there'd be one less to worry about, maybe even the one that's doing all the killing."

Garrett couldn't help but glance at Tora. She smiled at him, but he could tell there was no joy behind it. She was worried. They were all worried. "That wolf is not the same one that's causing the problem here," he said.

Fatias crossed his arms. "How do you know that?"

How did *he know that?* He couldn't very well tell the truth, and it wasn't in his nature to lie. So all he said was "I just know, that's all."

A small laugh coursed through the crowd.

"I say it's the logging companies!" Gavin Filmore said. He was an older man who'd moved to Redstone from Toronto. He'd come west to enjoy the forests and was against cutting down trees.

Michael Bines, the president of one of the smaller logging firms based in Redstone, stood up. "How is it the logging companies' fault? We employ more than half the people in this town, and the other half lives off the money that's earned by the first half."

"If you weren't cutting down so many trees," Gavin said, "the wolves wouldn't have to come so close to town for food."

A few people agreed with him, but they were shouted down by the loggers in the room.

"We cut only what we're allowed," Michael Bines said. "Pine beetles are killing off the rest . . . or maybe you want to blame us for that too."

The pine beetle was devastating British Columbia's forests, turning whole stands of lush green trees into dry red deadwood. The beetles were a natural enough phenomenon, but years of warmer winters had allowed the insects to spread, unchecked by nature. They were wiping out the forestry industry and people were looking for someone to blame.

"Maybe it *is* your fault," Gavin Filmore said.

Michael Bines and the rest of the loggers got up out of their chairs, looking to settle the matter with their fists.

Mayor Magill banged his gavel against the podium, taking charge of the meeting once more. "Settle down, people!" he shouted. "Settle down! This situation is nobody's fault. Man and nature are coming up against each other. It happens all the time, especially in a place like Redstone that's smack dab in the middle of one of the greatest forests on Earth. It's natural is all."

"Nothing natural about what I seen, Mayor Magoo!" someone catcalled from the back.

"These are mean, sick wolves," someone else said. "*Monster* wolves!"

That got the crowd going again.

"Shoot 'em all," another one said. "If we've got a wolf problem, we should just get rid of 'em."

"Bounty of a hundred dollars a tail would do it," someone else chimed in.

"Hundred an ear!"

"Make it a paw, and I'll start wolf hunting full-time!"

Ranger Brock felt sick to his stomach. There were plenty of laws against hunting wildlife such as wolves, but he knew as well as anyone that laws could be changed, amended, or even ignored. If everyone in town banded together in the hunt, the law would be almost powerless to stop them.

"Quiet down!" the mayor said, banging his gavel against the podium again. "Before we make any rash decisions, I think we should hear from Ranger Brock and Sergeant Martin about what steps they're taking to ensure the safety of our citizens." The mayor turned to Garrett. "Ranger Brock."

Garrett, smiling politely at the mayor, approached the podium. The room was quiet again, in anticipation. He'd checked the forest ranger's manual on the off chance there was something in it about wild werewolves, but he'd found it woefully lacking.

"What's being done," he said, stalling for time.

"Yeah," someone shouted. "What're you doing?"

He took a breath. "We've set a series of traps at the edge of town. When we have this pack's alpha male, we'll move it north, away from population. The rest of the wolves will follow."

"That's it?" came a call from the back of the room. "We're losing our pets, livestock, and maybe even our children, and you're playing catch and release?"

Another round of catcalls and jeers.

"I have to know my loggers are safe in the forest," Michael Bines said. "I can't send crews out to work in wolf-infested forests."

The ranger thought that was funny, considering that even a full-grown werewolf was no match for a logger with a high-powered chainsaw.

"I've already had half a dozen guests check out of my lodge early," Terry Houghton said. He and his wife, Halina, owned the Redstone Lodge on the eastern slope of the mountain. "After a woman from Vancouver said she saw a wolf out on Whitecap Run, that's all anyone in the lodge wanted to talk about. Business won't be good if people think the forest is swarming with killer wolves."

"Hear, hear," someone said.

Mayor Magill managed to get the room settled down enough to address the crowd. "I think we're all getting a little too excited here," he said. "Sure we've got animals in our forest. Lots of them. And if someone sees a wolf while they're out skiing, maybe you should charge them extra for it."

That got a laugh from the crowd.

But the mayor pushed his luck, saying, "I know for a fact that the woods are safe. And I plan on going for a walk in the forest tonight, after this meeting, to prove it."

"Sit down!" someone cried.

"Redstone might be better off if you went for a walk . . . and didn't come back!"

"Who said that?" shouted the mayor.

At this point, Sergeant Martin rose from his seat and approached the podium. The hall settled down quickly to hear the RCMP's take on the situation.

But before the sergeant spoke, he motioned for Garrett to join him. The ranger moved to the sergeant's side.

"Ranger Brock and I," he began, "are doing everything in our power to make Redstone safe. This is obviously a new situation for us and we need you to stay indoors and be patient."

"We'll give you some time," Terry Houghton said. "But not much."

"I ain't gonna wait," someone else said. "If I see a wolf, I'm gonna shoot it dead."

The sergeant put up his hands to calm the crowd. "The last thing we need is for people to take matters into their own hands. If anyone here kills a wolf, it'll be considered poaching and you will be prosecuted to the full extent of the law."

"Lotta good the law did for my dog," said Ernie Ilson. "I'll tell you what . . . I've got a hunting rifle and I intend to do me a little hunting. I'll be shooting for deer and rabbit, but if I end up hitting a wolf . . ." Shrug.

The crowd got to their feet, noisier than ever.

Amid the clamor, Garrett leaned over and said to the sergeant, "I've got a feeling this is going to get ugly."

"Yeah," the sergeant sighed. "And somebody in this room is going to get hurt before it's over."

The ride home seemed to take longer than it should have. The ranger sat silently behind the wheel, staring ahead at something far, far down the road. Every once in a while, he would move his hands on the steering wheel as if he were losing his grip, as if the car and everything around him might slip away if he weren't careful.

No one dared to say a word. The pack had never seen the ranger like this.

Thankfully, it was the ranger himself who broke the silence. "I don't want you running through the forest anymore," he said, his eyes still focused sharply on the road ahead.

"Not at all?" asked Tora.

The ranger took a deep breath, then said, "At least for a little while. Some of the people in town are. . . ," he searched for the word, "crazy for guns. They are going to be shooting first and asking questions later. They'll be looking for wolves, which is enough of a concern right there, but I know they'll end up shooting at anything that moves and that's what scares me most. Somebody is going to get hurt and I don't want it to be any of you."

Noble wanted to tell the ranger they could run in the forests far from town, but how could he question the man when he had their safety foremost in his mind?

"But we *have* to run," said Harlan. "It's who we are. It's in our blood."

"I know that," said the ranger. "And I'm sorry, but it's too dangerous for you – for anybody – to be out in the forest right now."

"Then what will we do in the meantime?" asked Tora.

"You'll just have to find something else."

The ranger's voice was loud and firm, and Noble knew that the matter was closed.

But Argus, who had been listening carefully with great interest, finally spoke up. "It's funny you should say that."

"Say what?"

"That we will have to find something else to do."

"It'll be only for a little while," the ranger said. "Until we get this mess straightened out."

"Well, today at school they put up a notice about the school's cross-country running team."

"And?" said the ranger, turning onto the last road that led to their home.

"Well. . . ," and here, Argus's voice began to falter, "I was wondering, if we're not allowed to run through the forest, maybe you'd let us run, you know, for the school."

The ranger said nothing.

Noble looked into the car's rearview mirror and saw the expression on the ranger's face. He seemed caught off guard by Argus's question.

"We'd be running on the track behind the school and on the streets in town," Argus said.

"Then why do they call it *cross-country*?"

Argus didn't have an answer. "I don't know."

"He would be running with other boys," Phyllis said.

"And girls," Tora chimed in.

"And you did tell them to find something else to do," Phyllis added.

The ranger sighed. "I just don't want them to make anyone look bad."

"I won't," said Argus.

"All right, okay. You can join the cross-country running team if you want," said the ranger, "but if you change form, or use any of your abilities to your advantage, it will be over."

Argus began bouncing up and down in his seat, as if he were grooving to some song on the radio. "Thank you," he said.

Noble whispered in Argus's ear, "What about your math marks?"

Argus put his hand over his mouth and said, "The ranger doesn't know yet."

Noble decided to say nothing more about it and to just let nature take its course.

Why had the man been so angry? the werewolf wondered, as he sat in a clearing deep in the forest, surrounded by the members of his pack. They had taken from him only what they needed, but the man did not want to share. Instead of letting them go on their way, the man had sent his dog to scare them off. Too bad . . . it had forced them to kill it. Such a brave and loyal animal did not deserve to die that way.

As if sending the dog to its death wasn't enough, the cowardly man had used his deathstick against them. The stick had boomed, and the crack had echoed across the mountain . . . but none of the pack had been hit.

It was a sign from Mother Earth that they were right to take what they needed from man. And with her blessing, they would be taking more.

For the winter's chill had brought the hunger once again.

He would feed the pack.

But this time he would not go to the place where men lived, but to the place where men went to get their food.

It would be safer that way.

Chapter 7

When Tora got to school, she went directly to her locker to put her books and lunch away, then headed out to look for Maria Abruzzo. Maria's mother had given her a new makeup kit and Maria'd offered to let Tora try some on before school.

Tora had never worn makeup before. It wasn't that Phyllis wouldn't let her, it was just that the topic had never really come up. With the exception of Phyllis, Tora was always surrounded by men, and when she was with her brothers, she did boy stuff. The pack's biggest thing was running through the forest and, in the past few months, they'd searched for a lost girl, fought a pack of wild wolves, scared off a crooked logging company, and saved the forest around Redstone. Before that, Tora had been captured by a mad doctor and held in a cage until her brothers were able to rescue her. Not exactly girl stuff.

Of course there had been the play, *Red Carnations*, in which Tora played a young woman. That was fun – dressing up in a costume, putting on theater makeup, and acting onstage – but Tora had been pretending to be someone older, someone prettier . . . someone else.

This was different.

Having a friend like Maria, a girlfriend, was something that Tora had been missing in her life. Trying on makeup, and even borrowing some of Maria's clothes, was a way for her to become something more than just Noble, Harlan, and Argus's little sister.

Maria was already in the bathroom when Tora entered. She had the makeup kit on the counter, next to one of the sinks, and was putting a bit of foundation on her cheek to cover up a blemish.

"Hey, Maria," Tora said.

Maria looked at Tora in the mirror. "Hey, there."

"What are you doing?"

Maria smiled. "I'm just using a bit of color to hide a pimple. I hate zits."

"Me, too," Tora said.

Maria turned around and looked at Tora's face. "You don't have any zits."

"I do too," Tora said, turning her head to the left and pointing to a pimple near her left ear.

"Well, what do you know." Maria dabbed some foundation onto Tora's cheek with a pad. "There," she said. "All gone."

Tora turned her head to look in the mirror. To her surprise, she couldn't see the pimple anymore. "Wow, thanks," she said.

"Here, try this," Maria said, handing Tora a lipstick.

Tora looked at it strangely, taking the tube in her hand as if it might break.

"It's just lipstick," Maria said, with a laugh. "It's not going to hurt you."

Tora fiddled with the tube, trying to bring the color out.

Maria reached over and gave the tube a twist. Suddenly a bright red bullet rose up. "Isn't this an awesome color?"

Tora nodded. It was so bright, so red . . .

Maria raised the lipstick to Tora's mouth and drew it gently across her lips. "There!"

Tora leaned in close to the mirror and took a good look at herself.

"Beautiful!" Maria said.

Tora smiled.

"Do you like it?"

"Yes." Tora liked the color red, not because it made her look pretty, but because it looked like she had the blood of a fresh kill on her lips.

"You should come over to my house sometime," Maria said. "You could try out my mascara, my blush . . . the works."

"I'd like that very much," Tora said, still looking at herself in the mirror.

At lunch, Tora and Maria met up in the same corner of the cafeteria and, this time, Tora had some chocolates in her bag in case Maria wanted to trade.

"So," Maria said. "Did anyone say anything?"

"About what?" Tora asked.

"Your lips. The lipstick."

"Oh, not really." A few boys had smiled in Tora's direction, but no one had actually said anything.

"What about Michael?"

"I haven't seen him, yet," Tora said. She felt badly that she hadn't been spending much time with her boyfriend lately, but that was offset by the excitement of having a girlfriend and discovering new things about herself.

"Hey, Tora, there you are!" came a voice from behind her.

She turned around to see Michael Martin. "Have a seat," she said, looking at Maria to make sure it was all right with her.

"I'd love to, thanks," he said, "but I've got to head to the library to study for a geography test. My marks are slipping and my dad's going to kill me if I get anything less than a seventy."

"He wouldn't do that," Tora said.

"He does have a gun, you know."

Tora and Maria laughed. Michael's father, a sergeant with the RCMP, did carry a gun, although no one in Redstone had ever seen him take it out of its holster.

"Good luck on your test, then," Tora said.

"Thanks."

"What are you doing Friday after school?" Maria asked.

Michael's eyes narrowed. "Thanks for asking, Maria," he whispered, "but I already have a girlfriend."

"Very funny," Tora said.

"We're thinking about going for pizza, then seeing that new horror movie."

"*Wolf Hounds of Death Creek*?"

"That's the one," said Maria.

"Noble, Argus, and Harlan are coming," Tora added.

"I'm *so* there," Michael said. He was about to leave when he stopped and stared at Tora. "Are you wearing lipstick?"

Tora could feel the blood rush to her face. "Yes."

"Looks good," he said. "See you Friday." He turned and left the cafeteria.

"You see," Maria said, smiling. "And the lipstick is almost gone."

Just then, Maria's other friends came into the cafeteria. As they approached their table, Maria waved. "Hey, guys, want to go for pizza and a movie after school Friday?"

"Sorry," said Gabriela Santos. "We've got plans."

"What kind of plans?" Maria wanted to know.

"I don't know," she said, with a shrug. "Just . . . plans."

The three girls walked past them and sat down several tables away, with another group.

"That's weird," said Maria. "We go for pizza and a movie all the time on Fridays."

"Maybe they *do* have plans," Tora offered.

Maria shook her head. "No, something's wrong."

The school day seemed to last a year for Argus. All he'd thought about through science, math, and English was running with the cross-country team after school. Ranger Brock had forbidden the pack to run, which had troubled Argus more than the others. He was the one who felt most at home in the forest. He loved the smell of it, the way the forest floor felt beneath his feet, the way the branches felt brushing against his fur, and, best of all, the thrill of hunting prey between the trees. Running through the forest was a big part of who Argus was. And while cross-country running as a human couldn't even come close, it was a decent substitute.

And so, Argus was the first one on the field after school, getting there even before Coach Quinn. Like the others, who began arriving a few minutes later, Argus wore a pair of red Redstone Secondary School shorts and a white Redstone T-shirt, both adorned with the Redstone Warriors logo (a stately representation of a Haida warrior, with a mountain over his right shoulder).

By the time Coach Quinn walked onto the field, the two dozen runners from the different grades were stretching and limbering up in anticipation of the run. Argus looked them all over carefully, dismissing the runners from the younger grades, then dismissing the rest because they were too fat, too skinny, or just plain goofy looking.

"Well, well, well," said Coach Quinn. "Argus Brock. I thought you weren't allowed on any school teams."

Argus smiled, flattered that Coach Quinn knew his name and some of his story.

"That was football, Coach. The ranger, I mean, my *dad*. . . ," Argus disliked using the word because the ranger was not his father, but people asked too many questions when he called the ranger anything else, "said I can't play any contact sports. But running's an individual thing, right?"

"Well," the coach said, hesitating, "this is the cross-country running *team*, but yes, you're basically on your own."

"Then I can do it?"

"Okay, I'm happy to have you on the team." He turned to face the others. "I'm happy to have all of you on the team."

The students came closer together, gathering around the coach.

"Unlike the other teams at Redstone Secondary, everyone who comes out to practice is on the cross-country team. All of you will be running at the races we compete in. So how well you do in this sport is up to you. I can help you with your breathing, and maybe some technique, but it basically comes down to how hard you work and how determined you are to improve yourself in the short time we have."

Everyone seemed buoyed by the coach's words.

None of the runners looked all that athletic to Argus and he imagined he could beat any of them in a race, easy. His problem, he figured, was how to win by just enough so as not to make anyone else look bad. He'd have to stay up to the leaders til near the end, then turn it on at the finish.

"All I ask is that you do your best," the coach continued. "The running season is short, and there's no point in coming out if you don't give it your all." A pause. "All right?"

"Yeah!" most of the runners said in unison, sprinkled with "All right!" and "Let's go, guys!"

"Now I'll show you our training course."

The runners closed in tighter on Coach Quinn as he showed them a map outlining the route they'd be running. Basically, they would be following the perimeter of Grenville and Davis Park, a public greenspace that backed onto the eastern edge of the school grounds. From where they were now, they'd run along the edge of the school parking lot, then over a large hill, down into a glen. Then it was up another hill, along a tree-lined ridge, down into a slight valley, through a mature forest, across another ridge, and then across the football field, back to where they started from.

"The route's about five kilometers long – a little longer than the distances you'll be running in competition and just long enough to make you competitive when we start racing. Any questions?"

Silence.

"Right. Is everyone ready? *Go!*"

Argus was caught off guard by the quick start and found himself about ten runners back before he'd taken twenty strides. To make up for it, he sprinted for a while, passing five runners before slowing to a comfortable jog next to the runner just four spots behind the lead.

"Hey, how are you doing?" Argus asked.

The runner beside him was Noel Nagleson, whose father worked as a clerk at the Big R department store in town. Noel didn't answer. Instead, he just kept running, breathing at a pace that matched the rhythm of his strides.

Argus shrugged, figuring that Noel, having trouble keeping pace, was pouring all of his concentration into his running. He decided to take it easy on the boy and match Noel's stride and breathing, step for step and breath for breath. But Argus had used up a large amount of energy sprinting from the back of the pack, and now he found that his lungs couldn't match Noel's regularly timed breaths. Instead Argus was panting like a dog, his mouth wide open as he gasped the way he always did on runs in his wolfen form, in-and-out, in-and-out. As a human on two legs, panting didn't seem to be working at all.

Slowly, a few inches at a time, Noel Nagleson pulled away from Argus, striding along like some thoroughbred horse – his breathing getting stronger, in-and-out, in-and-out, in-and-out, and his body showing no signs of tiring.

For the first time, Argus thought that he might not win this race. The idea nearly stopped him cold. It was unthinkable. He was Argus, the strongest and fastest werewolf in all of the forests around Redstone, probably in all of British Columbia. He would finish second to no one, let alone some teenage human boy.

Argus sprinted forward again, passing Noel and closing the distance on Spencer Houghton, a boy he knew from art class who once had a crush on Tora. Spencer was all legs, knees, and elbows, and he was running as if he'd seen a ghost. Spencer was a strong runner and Argus had trouble keeping pace.

They were on the first ridge now and Argus was able to take a look around. Behind him were a dozen or so runners, strung out along the path. In front were four others, one of whom was a girl. *This isn't happening,* he thought. Not only was he not leading the run, but there was a girl in front of him. *A girl!*

Again Argus sprinted forward, passing Spencer Houghton and leaving just three runners ahead. Directly in front was Kyan Houghton, Spencer's older brother, and another goofy-looking teenager who Argus should be toying with. Instead, Argus was gasping for air, his lungs feeling as if they might burst at any moment.

And they were only halfway through the race. Argus did his best to control his breathing, making it as even and regular as he could. That seemed to help. While he wasn't gaining on the second Houghton brother, he wasn't losing any distance. If he could just hang on for a while, maybe he could overtake him for third place.

A few minutes later, Argus had his chance.

They'd left the ridge and were running downhill toward the valley. Past the valley, the course wound through a forest and it was there that Argus felt he could make up the most ground on the runners in front of him.

The moment he entered the forest, his surroundings gave him strength. In his wolfen form, he could almost run forever through the trees. As a human, it was practically the same. His breathing became easier, his strides longer, and if he tried to go faster, his body responded.

Darting through the trees, Argus came up behind Kyan Houghton, matching his pace for ten strides or so, then bounding past him.

"Go, Argus, go!" Kyan cried.

What? Argus thought. *Why would he be cheering me on?* Argus put the thought behind him.

Now there were only two more runners ahead of him – Shannon Boersma, the girl, and Ronnie Camacho, another tall skinny kid who had no business being in the lead.

But they were out of the forest now and the strength Argus had felt running through the trees was all but gone. The fatigue in his chest, legs, and arms returned and he was again gasping for every breath.

Argus followed Shannon up the slope toward the top of the ridge. He was able to get close to her briefly, when she stumbled on a branch, but then she pulled away from him, tearing up the slope and across the ridge.

Argus did his best to catch up, sprinting when he had the energy and running wildly toward the finish line.

"Twenty-four, seventeen," Coach Quinn called out, as Argus crossed the line.

"Is that good?" Argus asked, falling to his knees. His whole chest heaved as he desperately tried to fill his lungs with air.

"Not bad," the coach answered. "It's third best today. Would probably put you in the top twenty at the provincial finals."

Third best? Argus thought. *Top twenty? No. No, no, no.* He was Argus Brock. He wasn't supposed to be third best or top twenty. He was number one, the best.

But as he knelt on the ground, bent over and struggling to catch his breath, both Shannon Boersma and Ronnie Camacho turned around and began running in the other direction.

"Where are they going?" Argus managed to say.

"Back to help the others," said Coach Quinn. "We're a team. Your race might be over, but theirs isn't."

Argus nodded. He would have loved to help the others finish the race . . . if he could.

"Next time," he said, between breaths.

Coach Quinn just laughed.

Chapter 8

After dinner, while the ranger and Phyllis went into Redstone to do some grocery shopping, Noble and Harlan sat down in front of the television and turned on their GameCube. They'd rented a new fighting game and wanted to get their money's worth before it had to be returned. Tora was in her room, talking on the phone with Michael Martin. Argus had left the dinner table and headed straight for his room. Now he emerged, dressed in a T-shirt and pair of shorts.

"Where are you going?" Noble asked, as Argus came down the hallway.

"Out for a run."

"What do you mean, 'out for a run'?" Noble asked.

"I'm going for a jog. No big deal."

Noble put down his controller in the middle of his game, giving Harlan an easy victory.

"Yeah!" Harlan cried out. Then, "Hey, what's going on?"

"Argus is going out for a run," Noble said.

Harlan rolled forward on the couch. "You can't do that."

"I can," said Argus. "And I will."

"But the ranger forbids it," Noble pointed out.

Argus hesitated, then said, "I'm not going against the ranger. He didn't want us out running *as wolves*. I'm going out as a human. I'm even wearing red and white. No one's going to mistake me for a wolf."

"I don't think it matters if you go running as a wolf *or* as a human. The ranger wants us to stay indoors, especially at night."

"I'll be back before dark. And I'll make sure I stay on the side of the road, away from the forest."

Noble got up and put himself between Argus and the front door. "I can't let you defy the ranger."

Argus stood tall, clenching his fists. "Do you want to fight me over this?"

Noble thought about it. *What on earth had made Argus want to ignore the ranger's orders, and now want to fight a brother over it?*

"Of course not," said Noble. He stared into his brother's eyes. "What's gotten into you? We don't fight over things like this."

Argus took a deep breath, but his shoulders slumped forward, as if some of his determination had gone. "I went out for the cross-country team today."

"And?"

"We had our first training run."

"How'd you do?"

It took Argus a while to answer. "*Third!*" he said, as if there were a big oily glob of sludge on his tongue.

"You didn't win?" Harlan asked, dumbfounded.

"No, I did not."

"Who beat you?"

"Ronnie Camacho."

"That skinny little nerd?" Harlan was grinning ear to ear.

"And Shannon Boersma."

"Shannon Boersma? She's a girl."

Argus rolled his eyes. "I know she's a girl. That's why I've got to practice running on two feet, so I can finish first."

Noble put a hand on Argus's shoulder. "Just because we're different – special, even – doesn't mean we're automatically the best at everything. There are a lot of good athletes at our school, and no matter how good we are at something, there will always be someone who is better, stronger, faster. . . ."

"Maybe," Argus said. "But that doesn't mean I can't try to be the best. Coming third has given me a challenge and I intend to rise to it." A pause. "Now, you can either fight me to keep me in the house, or you can step aside and let me do what I've got to do."

Noble thought about it, then stepped aside.

"Thank you," Argus said.

When Argus was gone, Harlan asked Noble, "Why'd you let him go?"

"Because I knew that I'd never be able to stop him."

They went to the front door and watched Argus jog down the drive toward the road.

"Is he crazy?" Harlan asked.

Noble shook his head. "There's just too much alpha male in Argus to let someone else win, even something as simple as a high school cross-country training run."

"But he lets you be the leader."

"*Lets* me be the leader is right. If he wanted to fight me for the leadership, he'd win, of course. But he knows that living in the human world requires more than brute strength. It requires a mind that can reason and use logic, and he knows he falls short on those. And after he beat the wild wolf pack's alpha male in that fight, he probably thought he was invincible. So when he was beaten today by a skinny, nerdy human and a girl, it must have come as quite a shock to him."

"Do you think he'll get over it?"

Noble watched Argus turn right off the drive and head out onto the road. "We can only hope."

The ranger and Phyllis returned from grocery shopping well after sundown. They hadn't planned on spending so much time there, but someone had broken into the Redstone IGA's meat locker overnight, and the manager wanted the ranger's opinion on who or what might have done it. The manager had tried to convince the ranger that it was the same wolves that had killed Ernie Ilson's dog, but the ranger just shook his head and said, "What kind of wolves break into meat lockers? It was probably kids, or some drunk, that's all."

The manager wasn't convinced, and it took the ranger and Phyllis almost an hour before they could start their shopping. And so, by the time they arrived back at the house, they were tired and eager to call it a night. They emptied out the car and headed inside, their arms full of shopping bags. The ranger had the added burden of a large case of diet cola.

"Is there anything left in the car?" Noble asked, as Phyllis placed her bags on the kitchen floor.

"No, that's it," she said. "Our money just doesn't buy as much as it used to."

"You can help put this stuff away, though," the ranger said, passing the case of soda to Harlan, while Tora busied herself with putting away bags of cookies and boxes of cereal.

The ranger took a look around. "Where's Argus?"

Harlan headed for the cold-storage room, pretending he hadn't heard. Tora opened and closed a few cupboards, seemingly confused about where things went. And Noble just kept searching in the shopping bags on the floor, as if the answer lay somewhere between the apples and the bags of milk.

"Okay," said the ranger. "Let me rephrase that . . . where is Argus?"

No answer.

"Noble?" the ranger asked.

There was no avoiding the question now, Noble realized, who, almost by virtue of his name, was bound to tell the ranger the truth.

"Uh," Noble said, looking up. "He sort of went out."

"Out? Where?" The ranger's voice was loud now, with a tone of urgency.

"Out," Noble said, pausing, "for a run."

"What?" The ranger's anger was now in full bloom. "I told *all of you* that I didn't want anyone running through the forest."

Noble was faced with a dilemma. He didn't want to rat on his brother, but he didn't want to protect him anymore either. He realized that he had no option but to tell the truth and let Argus deal with the ranger's wrath.

"He didn't go out running as a wolf," Noble said, at last.

Phyllis breathed a sigh of relief. The ranger was also visibly relieved, but all he said was "And?"

"At the cross-country training run today, he finished third. . . . He wanted to get in some extra training."

"And you let him go?"

"I tried to stop him," Noble said, angry that Argus had put him in this situation.

"He did," said Tora.

"That's right," echoed Harlan.

"But he was determined to go, and he convinced himself that it would be okay with you," said Noble.

The ranger said nothing.

"What was I supposed to do?" Noble asked. "Fight him?"

The question hung in the air like smoke. The ranger finally shook his head and said, "No, I guess not."

Phyllis grabbed a jar of peanut butter and put it away in a cupboard. "How long ago did he leave?"

Noble glanced at the kitchen clock. "It's been a while. He should be home anytime now."

"All right," said the ranger, lifting a bag off the floor. "We'll deal with this when he gets back."

They all emptied the shopping bags and put things away in the refrigerator, cupboards, and pantry as well as in the cold room downstairs.

Suddenly the sound of a gunshot echoed off the mountain.

Everyone stopped and listened.

And then, in the silence, the ranger whispered, "Argus!"

A half hour later, it was dark. The ranger had been on the phone for most of that time, trying to track down Sergeant Martin. He'd sent the rest of the pack down the drive to check the roadway, but they'd come back reporting that Argus was nowhere to be seen. Phyllis had used their cell phone to call the hospital, but no one – especially anyone named Argus Brock – had been brought in with a gunshot wound.

Ranger Brock dialed the RCMP number again and, this time, a constable picked up the phone.

"RCMP Redstone, Constable Neavis speaking," the man said.

"This is Garrett Brock. I'm a forest ranger here in –"

"I know who you are, Mr. Brock," the constable said.

"I want to speak to Sergeant Martin. Do you know where he is?"

"He's out on a call right now. Ernie Ilson shot at a wolf, creeping behind his place."

The ranger felt the blood drain from his face. His knees were weak. He searched behind him for a chair to sit down on. "Do you know if he hit the wolf?"

"Said he did, but he can't find the animal. The sergeant's out there right now, helping him look for it."

Ranger Brock took a deep breath. At least the wolf was still alive, somewhere out in the forest. An image of Argus, shot and bleeding, perhaps even dying from traces of silver poisoning in his body, clouded his mind, terrifying him to his core.

"Ranger Brock? Are you still there?"

The sound of the constable's voice startled the ranger. "Yes, yes I am."

"Do you still want to reach the sergeant?"

The ranger could barely manage the word. "Yes."

"I'll have him call you."

The ranger hung up.

"Is it Argus?" Phyllis asked, her fisted hands tucked carefully beneath her chin.

"Probably," answered the ranger. Then, "Maybe." And finally, "I don't know."

Phyllis rushed to the ranger's side and put her arms around him. Then she started to cry.

At that point, the back door opened.

Argus stood in the doorway, drenched in sweat.

Everyone stared at him.

"What?" Argus asked.

"Where on earth have you been?" the ranger said, his voice strangely loud.

"I, uh, I just went out for, uh –"

"Ranger Brock!" Harlan interrupted. "I think you should come and see this."

The ranger glared at Argus. Finally he went to where Harlan was standing. "What is it?" he said.

"Look," Harlan answered, pointing into the backyard.

Phyllis and the rest of the pack went to the window that overlooked the yard. "Oh, no," she said.

Noble and the others just stared. No one said a word.

Illuminated by the porch light, in the middle of the yard stood a huge silver-gray werewolf. There was no mistaking its coloration. This had to be the alpha male Argus had fought in the clearing to save Angelina Abruzzo, only now it was in its full werewolf form.

Seven feet of tangled fur and rippling muscle, arms like tree branches, legs like stumps. It stood erect and proud, its mouth open. Its face had a strange expression of anger and sorrow. And its eyes . . . its eyes looked wet and glassy, as if the animal were trying to shed a tear, but couldn't.

All of this, because of the wolf in its arms.

Blood was dripping from its leg, where buckshot had torn into its hindquarter. The animal's head was lolling left and right, and its eyes were open, blank, and lifeless.

Harlan was the first to speak. "What does it want?"

"It wants our help," the ranger said, rushing to get a bunch of clean towels from a kitchen drawer.

"But how did it know to come here?"

"Maybe it knows I'm a forest ranger, or that you four live here." He cut two of the dish towels with a pair of scissors and tore them into strips, then headed toward the back door. "The important thing is, it's here now and it needs our help to save that wolf."

The ranger stood for a moment in the doorway.

The werewolf's body tensed in a *fight or flight* response.

"It's okay," the ranger said. "I can help."

Slowly, the werewolf relaxed a little, but it remained where it was, holding the dying wolf close to its chest.

"But I can't do anything unless you trust me," the ranger said, still in the doorway.

Noble looked past the ranger, over to the werewolf in the yard. There was no sign that the silver-gray beast understood what the ranger was saying, but it did seem to be responding to his tone of voice.

The ranger left the safety of the house and took two steps out into the yard.

The werewolf did not move.

The ranger took two more steps and suddenly they were less than ten feet apart.

The werewolf nudged the head of the wolf in its arms with its snout. The wolf responded with a slight jerk of its head.

"It's still alive!" Tora shouted.

The ranger moved forward slowly, motioning with his hands for the werewolf to put the wolf down.

Somehow the animal understood. It knelt down, first on one knee, then the other. Gently it placed the fallen wolf onto the grass.

Ranger Brock slowly approached, placing a hand on the wolf's neck to check for a pulse. Then he took several of the cloth strips from around his neck and tied off the wolf's leg to stop the bleeding.

Turning back to face the house, he said, "Call Doctor Katz."

Noble turned around and saw that Phyllis was already on the phone. "He says he's having dinner at the moment," she said.

"You tell him, I don't care if he's at the table with the queen, he's got to get here NOW!" said the ranger.

Phyllis repeated the ranger's instructions, then hung up. "He's on his way," she said.

"Good," Ranger Brock said. He put a hand on the wolf's head and petted the animal comfortingly. With any luck, the doctor would be there in ten or fifteen minutes.

Noble went to the door. "What will we do when he gets here?" he asked.

The ranger looked from the wolf lying on the ground to the werewolf kneeling on the grass before him. "All right," he said. "Argus, Noble, and Harlan, give me a hand moving the wolf into the garage. Phyllis and Tora, spread a few blankets over the hood of the car. . . . And when the doctor gets here, make sure he comes straight into the garage."

Noble and his brothers went out into the yard.

Seeing them, the silver-gray werewolf crawled backward to the edge of the yard, until it was crouched next to a big cedar and half-hidden by a stand of saplings.

"On three," said the ranger.

The pack moved into position around the wolf.

"One."

Noble firmed his grip around the wolf's neck.

"Two."

The wolf was a limp thing in his hands, as if all of the life had been drained from its being.

"Three."

All four of them lifted together, and Noble was surprised at how much of a deadweight the wolf was.

They walked in unison into the garage and placed the animal down on top of the car. A few seconds passed before they all took a breath.

"Do you think it will live?" Argus asked.

"Let's hope so," the ranger said, glancing out one of the garage windows at the werewolf, still sitting steadfast between the trees. "For our sake, and the sake of the town."

Noble didn't quite understand. "What about the one out there?"

The ranger shook his head. "It's trusting us for now." He put a hand on the wolf's head and stroked it. "This is probably the werewolf's mate. If she dies, the werewolf will be sad, but eventually it'll find another. Worse than that, it'll be angry. *Mad*, in every sense of the word. Humans will have killed its mate, and it might want to exact its revenge against every man, woman, and child in Redstone."

A shiver chilled its way down Noble's spine. He went back to the kitchen and glanced at the clock. "Where's Doctor Katz?" he said. "Shouldn't he be here by now?"

Chapter 9

The werewolf stayed hidden between the trees, near where the man lived. Over the years, the animals of the forest had come to know that the man here was different. Better, somehow . . .

He wore colors created by Mother Earth. He never carried a deathstick. And he was known not to have ever harmed one from the forest. Furthermore, several creatures injured by Mother Earth had found their way to this place, were taken in by the man, then let go when they were made better.

The female wolf had been felled by a deathstick, and not by Mother Earth, but if the man had healing powers, then he could use them here as well. At least here, there was a chance. . . .

The werewolf closed its eyes, exhausted. It was part man now, and with its new form came many new burdens.

Before, as leader, there were few things he had to worry about beyond food, shelter, and survival of the pack. Now that he walked on two legs, his head was full of *thoughts*.

When the change first came over him, he had savored the idea of being *man*, but as the days passed and he spent more time near the places men lived, he wanted less and less to do with them.

When the female had fallen, his first instinct had been to kill the man who had hurt her, rip him apart and feast on his flesh. But the man had a deathstick, and even if he killed him, it would only anger other men with deathsticks. They would seek out the pack and kill them.

No, even though he walked on two legs, he was not man, nor could he ever be. It had been wrong to think otherwise. And the more he *thought* about it, the more he knew that he did not want to be any more like man than he already was.

When the female was well again – and somehow he knew that the man who lived here could make it so – he would take her and his pack deep into the forest, where his newfound abilities would make him a better leader. His pack would prosper and he would never need to get so close to man again.

The silver-gray werewolf's eyes remained closed and its head lowered. It drifted off into a shallow and fitful sleep, its mind haunted by thoughts of deathsticks and survival. . . . And getting as far away from man as it could.

Doctor Katz was an older man with a slight build, thinning salt-and-pepper hair, and an infectious smile. He'd been the veterinarian in Redstone for close to forty years and had treated generation after generation of the town's pets, livestock, and wildlife. He'd seen everything, or so he thought.

"First time I've ever treated a wild animal on the hood of a car in someone's garage," he said, wiping at the wolf's hind leg with a clean cloth, then injecting her with a sedative to keep her still. "Why is it you had me come all the way out here instead of bringing the animal to my office?" he asked.

Doctor Katz had already asked that question, but Ranger Brock wasn't about to tell the doctor the truth, no matter how hard the man fished for it.

"I thought the animal was badly hurt," he said, not mentioning the huge werewolf hiding out in his backyard. "And I didn't want to risk moving her. With the condition of some of our roads, I was convinced the ride into town would kill her."

Doctor Katz looked at Ranger Brock for several long moments. The ranger had always felt that the doctor was aware of the pack's secret and that he asked questions in an attempt to discover the truth. If the doctor saw any signs of deception on the ranger's face, the ranger would never know. The doctor merely muttered an "uh-huh," then focused his attention on the wolf.

"There's *a lot* of buckshot here," he said, sliding his glasses up the bridge of his nose. "I stopped counting after fifteen."

"Can you get them out?" the ranger asked.

"It will take some time and a little digging, but I think so," the doctor responded.

"So it's not as bad as it looks?"

The doctor took out an electric shaver to cut back the wolf's fur and give himself clean patches of skin to work on. He handed the end of its cord to Harlan, who was standing by along with the other members of the pack. "Plug that in, please," he said.

Harlan plugged the shaver into an extension cord and then uncoiled the cord until it reached the socket by the side door.

"Doctor," Ranger Brock said again. "So it's not that bad? The wolf's going to make it?"

The doctor tested the shaver by switching it on and taking a close look at the blades. Then he glanced at the ranger. "The wolf will live. I'll remove the buckshot, close up her wounds, and give her some medication, but I'll have to take her with me so I can monitor her healing for a few days."

The ranger did his best to remain calm and keep his face expressionless. "I'd prefer you didn't," he said.

"You want the animal to recover, don't you?" the doctor asked.

"Of course."

"She can't be released into the forest until I'm sure her wounds have sufficiently healed."

"I understand," said the ranger.

"Then she should board with me for a few days."

"No!" said the ranger. His tone was firm and unwavering. "I have pens behind the garage. The wolf will stay here. You can visit as often as you need to."

The doctor's eyes narrowed. "One day," he said, "you'll tell me what's going on here."

The ranger said nothing.

"One day," the doctor repeated, "but not today."

The ranger let out a sigh.

The doctor returned his attention to the wolf and switched on the shaver.

Ranger Brock moved slowly over to the window and looked out.

The werewolf was still there, barely illuminated by the porch light, patiently waiting for its mate to be well again.

"Should we go out there?" Tora said, looking out the living-room window at the werewolf, just beyond the edge of their backyard. The ranger had asked them to leave the garage while the doctor worked.

"It would be neat to get to know it," Harlan said.

"No!" Noble said. "The ranger was clear . . . we're not to go near it."

"Why not?" asked Argus. "It's one of us."

Noble looked at his bigger brother, wondering what was wrong with him these days. He'd ignored the problems he was having in math class, defied the ranger's decision forbidding them from running through the forest, and now he questioned the ranger's wisdom about keeping them away from this new werewolf.

"No, it's not one of us." Noble said. "It's a wild animal. The ranger was clear on that point."

"If it's so wild, then how did it know to bring the injured wolf here?" Argus said. "To our house, of all the houses on the mountain?"

Noble had wondered that himself. "I don't know," he said. "Maybe the animals understand this is a place where a good man lives. Or maybe becoming a werewolf made him that much smarter." He threw up his hands in frustration. "Who knows. The only thing that matters is that the ranger asked us not to go out there. And I happen to agree with him."

"Really?" said Argus.

"Yes," Noble answered. "You might be able to approach it, or maybe even speak to it. But what if something bad happens? There's no telling what that werewolf might do. What if it gets spooked, or recognizes you as the one who nearly killed it out in the forest? What if it decides it would like a rematch? Are you going to fight it in the backyard, werewolf against werewolf, while Doctor Katz is still out in the garage?"

Argus silently stared out the window at the werewolf.

Noble studied Argus's reflection in the glass. There was a streak of defiance growing within Argus, defiance against himself and against the ranger. Unchecked, it might continue to grow until something very bad happened, or someone was seriously hurt.

Noble hoped it would never come to that.

Two hours went by before Doctor Katz was finished.

After removing twenty-three pieces of buckshot, he'd taken a battery-powered metal detector from his bag and waved it back and forth over the wolf's leg. The wand, looking like a beaver's tail with a handle on one end, had chirped and beeped several times until the doctor had been able to narrow down where the last piece of buckshot was hidden.

"Okay, I see it," he said, then folded back a flap of skin and removed a pie-shaped shard of metal, round on one end and sharpened to a point at the other.

The ranger and the doctor both looked at the piece for a long time.

"It looks like a quarter of a quarter," said the ranger, at last.

"Maybe it's a *silver* quarter," the doctor added. He turned the piece over, then wiped away the blood with his thumb. "Here's the date it was minted – 1969."

The ranger breathed a sigh of relief. Silver quarters were last made by the Royal Canadian Mint in 1968, when they were half silver and half copper. Since then, quarters have been made primarily out of nickel, and, most recently, steel. Ernie Ilson had the right idea peppering his buckshot with bits of silver; he'd just gotten the year wrong. But Ranger Brock wasn't going to mention any of that to the doctor. Instead, he just said, "Isn't that strange?"

"Quite," said the doctor. "I can't think why anyone would go to the trouble of putting a piece of silver quarter in a shotgun shell. . . ," he looked directly at the ranger, "can you?"

The ranger simply shrugged.

A follow-up check with the metal detector showed that the wolf was clear of buckshot, so the doctor began to clean and dress the wound.

When he was done, the wolf's leg and hindquarter were wrapped neatly in white gauze and bandages. A few spots of blood had leaked through, but the doctor said it was normal until the wounds scabbed over.

"So she's going to be all right?" asked the ranger.

The doctor stroked the animal from head to tail, as if treasuring the chance to be in such close contact with a wild animal. "She's lucky none of her bones were broken. I don't think she would have put up with a cast long enough for her leg to heal."

"How soon can we let her back into the forest?"

"How on earth should I know?" Doctor Katz said. "I'm a veterinarian, not a fortune-teller."

"Would you hazard a guess?"

The doctor lifted his hands and shrugged. "She might want to leave as soon as she wakes up, or in a day or so after she's had some food and clean water. . . . Since you're not letting me take the animal with me, and I can't be sure of my schedule in the next few days, I'll leave it up to the wolf."

"The wolf?"

The doctor nodded. "She'll let you know when she's strong enough to leave, but if I had to guess, I'd say that if there's no sign of infection, you could probably set her free on Friday."

"Friday's good," said the ranger. While the werewolf behind his house seemed patient enough now, he wondered if it might still be that way once the wolf was up and walking.

"Let me help you get her into the pen, then I'll be on my way."

"We can manage," the ranger said. "You've been kind enough already, coming out here and letting her stay with us. We'll carry her outside. You get back to your family."

"If you insist," the doctor said, packing up his bag.

"I'll walk you to your car," said the ranger. He escorted the doctor out of the garage and shook his hand. "Thank you," he said.

The doctor sighed. "It is my job, but you're welcome just the same." He then tipped his hat and walked down the driveway to his car.

When Ranger Brock heard the doctor pull away from the house, he called the others into the garage to help him carry the wolf to the pens out back.

"Is she going to be all right?" Tora asked, as the ranger and the pack grabbed the edges of the blanket and lifted the wolf off the hood of the car.

"The doctor said she should be fine," he grunted, while wrestling with the weight of the animal.

"How long before we can let her go?" Harlan asked.

"A day or two."

They were outside now and Phyllis ran ahead to open the gate of the first pen.

"Careful," the ranger said, as they eased the animal onto the ground. "As close to the fence as possible."

They all pulled together until the wolf was directly against the fence.

"Now what?" Noble asked.

"She should be waking up any minute now. We'll put some food out and . . . well, wait, I guess."

They left the pen, one by one, then turned around to look at the wolf. She was asleep, breathing easy and at peace.

The ranger looked for the werewolf, but it was gone. "C'mon," he said. "Let's get inside."

They all headed toward the house.

"And, Argus," said the ranger, "don't think I've forgotten about this little run you went on."

"But I stayed close to the road," Argus said.

"We'll talk about it inside."

"Yes, ranger."

They all entered the house, and the door closed shut behind them.

Several minutes passed. Then a silver-gray figure moved out of the forest like a shadow, until it came to a stop outside the pen behind the garage. It sniffed at the fallen wolf, then reached through the fencing until it could touch its mate.

The wolf on the ground stirred. Her eyes fluttered open.

The werewolf pulled back its hand, crouched down by

the fence and nodded, as if it somehow knew that everything was going to be all right.

Garrett Brock made himself comfortable in his favorite chair in the living room, took a sip of the coffee Phyllis had made for him, then said, "Argus, can you come here, please?"

The house went quiet. The only sound was the squeak and groan of the wooden floorboards under Argus's feet as he came down the hall into the living room.

When he appeared, Garrett studied Argus's face – the lines on it were straight and sharp, suggesting a physical strength that the ranger could never have himself. Argus was strong and muscular, with broad shoulders, and the rest of the world would look upon him as already a man.

But Garrett knew better.

Despite his size and strength, Argus had a long way to go before becoming an adult. Garrett wondered how to convince him – a hulking teenage werewolf – that he still had to follow the rules.

"Have a seat," he instructed Argus.

Argus sat down opposite the ranger.

"What were you doing out running?"

"You said I could run."

"I said you could join the school running team."

"But if I'm going to be on the team, I have to practice."

Garrett nodded. "But don't they have practice after school?"

Argus said nothing and looked away. Finally, he mumbled, "Yeah, we practiced."

Garrett immediately knew something had gone wrong. "Somebody beat you in practice, didn't they?" he guessed. "You didn't finish first."

Argus's jaw dropped open. "How did you know?"

Garrett couldn't help but smile. "Phyllis and I have raised you four since you were pups. We know everything about you. Even more than you know yourself."

Argus sighed. "I came in third."

Garrett was surprised at that. *Third!* What a shock it must have been for Argus, who had always been the strongest and fastest at everything. No wonder he wanted to do more running.

"Third is still good," Garrett said.

"For someone else, maybe," Argus replied, his teeth slightly clenched. "But not for me . . . and not when one of the people in front of me is a girl."

"Okay," Garrett said, a few moments later. "Obviously you want to do well at this cross-country thing."

"Yes."

"And you can probably use as much practice as you can get running as a human."

"Uh-huh."

"So I will allow you to run –"

"All right!"

"But only under the following conditions."

Argus's eyes were open wide in anticipation.

"You run only in daylight hours and only along the main roads. . . ."

"No problem."

"And, you keep up with all your schoolwork."

Argus hesitated slightly, but then said, "I can do that."

"Good," the ranger said, extending his hand. "Then we have a deal."

Argus reached out and the two shook hands.

"You won't let me down."

"No," Argus said, with a bit of a laugh. "You know me."

"Yes, I do," Garrett said. "And that's why I'm worried."

Later that evening, the phone rang. Ranger Brock heard it, but didn't bother getting up from his chair. The day's events had left him extremely tired, and it was probably somebody calling for one of the boys, or Michael Martin calling to say good night to Tora, or maybe even Tora's new best friend, Maria Abruzzo, calling to say, "You'll never guess who said hello to me in the hallway today. . . ."

"Garrett."

The ranger turned to see his wife, Phyllis, standing in the living room with the phone in her hand.

"Who is it?"

"Konrad Martin."

"What does he want?"

"He wants to talk to you."

The ranger slowly rose to his feet. He hoped the sergeant had good news, but there was something troubling in the pit of his stomach.

He took the phone. "Hello?"

"Sorry to call you so late," said Sergeant Martin.

"Not a problem," said the ranger. "What's the matter?"

"It's Ernie Ilson again."

"What is it now?"

"He had a talk with Doctor Katz. He's upset that he shot that wolf fair and square and you went and saved its life."

"But I'm a forest ranger, it's what I do."

"Yeah, well. He wants it killed. He's been on the blower to all of his redneck friends and now they're on board with him. They all want the wolf dead."

Garrett shook his head. "That's crazy. Nobody's going to kill anything."

"I figured you'd feel that way, but they do have a point, you know."

"And what point is that?"

"Well, after this wolf is better and you relocate it back in the forest, what's to stop it from coming and attacking their property and animals again?"

"That won't happen," said Garrett.

"How do you know?"

There was no way to predict what the injured wolf and the werewolf might do from day to day. But judging by what he'd seen of the werewolf, the ranger had a strong feeling that when all of this was over, the werewolf would be taking his pack as far away from Redstone as possible.

"I just know, that's all."

"You mean, like a hunch?" asked the sergeant.

"You could say that."

"Well, if that's all you've got, you're going to have to convince them of it yourself."

"Not another town meeting."

"No, there are only six or seven of them now who are out for the wolf's blood. The rest are happy to know that it was shot and is going to be moved."

"All right," Garrett said, with a sigh. "When and where?"

"How about here at the detachment tomorrow afternoon?"

"I'll be there."

"Good, I'll let them know."

Garrett hung up the phone, wondering when these people would be satisfied.

It was a no-win situation.

Chapter 10

As usual, Argus wasn't looking forward to math class. Before school, he'd met up with a few classmates and convinced them to let him copy their homework. He didn't understand it, but it looked as if he did, and that's about all Argus was worried about. Each day was another day closer to the end of the year.

"Right," said Mr. Surujpaul, as he entered the room. "Everyone do their homework last night?"

The class answered all at once with a mix of responses.

"Ayris, did you?" he asked a girl in the back row.

"Yes," she answered. A teacher's daughter, Ayris Oakland was the class brain.

"What about you, Nathan?"

"I think I did it," Nathan answered.

Everyone laughed.

"And what about Mr. Tomat?"

Cliff Tomat was a local hockey star. "No," he said, shaking his head. "I didn't have time. Last night's game was in Prince George and we didn't get back til late."

Mr. Surujpaul frowned, but said nothing. Instead he turned to Argus. "I suppose you did your homework, Argus?"

Argus nodded and opened his notebook to the pages he'd copied that morning.

Mr. Surujpaul looked at the work a moment and said, "Good, then you shouldn't have any trouble with a pop quiz."

A collective groan arose from the class.

"Don't worry," said Mr. Surujpaul. "The quiz mark won't be used to determine your final mark. It's only to give me an idea of where you all are."

Suddenly the tension in the room was gone and everyone relaxed.

Everyone except Argus.

Argus could feel the room getting hot and his face getting red. He was looking at a failing mark, maybe a zero. And even if the quiz didn't count toward his overall grade, a poor score would tell Mr. Surujpaul that he hadn't really done his homework and had been lying.

"It shouldn't take you more than fifteen minutes," said Mr. Surujpaul, as he handed out the quiz.

Argus took a quick look around, then shifted his desk a few inches to his right, closer to Ayris's desk.

Mr. Surujpaul placed the test on Argus's desk and moved on down the row.

Argus took a look at it.

Nothing. His mind was a blank. Sweat dampened his clothes. Maybe he could take math again in summer school, but the thought made him sigh. He loved spending the summer in the forest, running and hunting all day and night. Summer school was unthinkable.

He took another look around and suddenly saw the way out he'd been hoping for. Ayris was left-handed and, as she did her work, Argus had a clear view of her answers.

Coolly, calmly, as if it were the most natural thing in the world, Argus shifted his entire body to the right, then looked at Ayris's paper. The first answer was there for him, clear as day. He looked away then – careful not to make it look as if he were cheating – and copied the answer onto his own paper.

He looked right again. Answer number two.

Again and again, he copied Ayris's work until they were both finished. But instead of putting his pencil down, Argus kept on scribbling, putting in phony corrections and intentionally getting one of the questions wrong.

"Okay, time's up," Mr. Surujpaul said. "Pass your quiz to the person in front of you. First person in the row, give your quiz to the person at the back."

Mr. Surujpaul went over the answers. Argus Brock had gotten every question right, but one.

Argus breathed a sigh of relief.

Another math class had come and gone.

Phyllis had spent the early part of the morning on the phone with Doctor Katz and then gone into Redstone to buy some fresh meat. Ground beef was a poor substitute for the fresh kill that the wolf was used to in the wild, but it was easy to eat and made hiding medicine and vitamins a snap. Now that she had prepared the wolf's meal, it was time to see if the animal was strong enough to eat it.

The moment Phyllis opened the door to the backyard, there was movement in the trees. She was startled by the noise of the werewolf darting back into the safety of the forest. "Poor thing," she said, under her breath. "It must be worried sick."

She wondered if the werewolf might want something to eat as well, since it hadn't moved from the backyard since it arrived. The least she could do was offer it some food and a bowl of water.

As she neared the pen, she found the injured wolf lying on her side by the fence closest to the forest. When the wolf heard Phyllis approaching, she slowly got up onto all fours and limped over to the door, where Phyllis would be entering.

"Better, I see," she said, opening the gate.

The wolf moved close to Phyllis, but still maintained some distance – perhaps out of respect, perhaps out of distrust. That suited Phyllis just fine. She put the large steel tray with food and water down onto the ground, then slowly exited the pen.

With the gate locked behind her, Phyllis stood there watching the wolf sniff at the food and eat it hungrily.

"Excellent," she said, clapping her hands together. The wolf was doing much, much better and in another day or two, she would likely be strong enough to leave. And no matter what the doctor said, the wolf could leave whenever she wanted to, thanks to the werewolf, who could tear open the fence whenever it pleased.

Phyllis scanned the woods for a sign of it. She was surprised to find the werewolf not hiding amid the trees, but sitting comfortably on the grass at the edge of the backyard.

Caught off guard and without thinking, Phyllis waved to it.

Even more surprising, the werewolf waved back. It was little more than a raised hand with only the slightest sideways movement, but the wild animal was quickly learning to interact with humans.

That was good, thought Phyllis. Coexisting with humans might be just the thing that would save its life and the lives of the rest of the wolves in its pack.

Phyllis waved at the werewolf once more, then hurried inside to call Garrett and tell him the good news.

Argus was the first member of the cross-country team on the field after school. This was the moment he'd been thinking about all day long. Another run. A chance to redeem himself. He could win today. He could feel it.

"Hey, Argus Brock," Coach Quinn said. "You came back?"

"What do you mean? I'm on the team, aren't I?"

"Yes, of course, but a lot of people come out to run with the team . . . once. When they realize how hard it is, they quit. We have only a couple of competitions each season, so you really have to like running to stay on the team."

"I love to run," Argus said.

"I can see that," replied the coach.

By now the rest of the team had arrived, including Shannon Boersma and Ronnie Camacho, the two who had beaten him the day before.

"Hey, Argus," said Ronnie.

"Hi, Argus," said Shannon.

They're so friendly, Argus thought. *I don't want to be their friend. I want to beat them!*

"All right," said Coach Quinn. "I think that's everyone. On your mark . . ." He blew his whistle and the runners headed out.

This time Argus made sure he was up at the front. By the first turn, he was with a group of four that included Ronnie, Shannon, and Shannon's little sister, Katelyn, a grade-nine student who hadn't been at practice the day before. But by the time they were heading up the first hill, Katelyn was dropping behind.

Throughout the middle of the run, Argus was content to keep pace with the other two runners, holding his tongue in his mouth and making sure his breathing was deep and steady. That was one thing he'd learned on his run the night before. Wolves panted when they ran and that suited them well, but it was all wrong for humans. While wolves cooled themselves by hanging their tongues out and panting, humans cooled off by sweating, leaving their mouths to breathe.

After they'd gone down the first valley and climbed the hill on the other side, Ronnie was obviously hurting. He was breathing hard and his hand was gripping his side like he was in pain. Argus would be assured of at least a second.

"Keep going, Argus," Ronnie said, as he slowed.

Argus laughed under his breath.

As he continued over the crest of the hill, Argus had only Shannon Boersma left in front of him. She was still running strong and showing no signs of slowing down. But Argus was feeling good and was sure he could pour it on before the finish line and put Shannon behind him.

Argus quickened his pace . . . and felt his lungs begin to ache. His legs and arms burned and it took everything he had to stay even with Shannon. When he pulled up next to her, she smiled.

She's smiling at me, Argus thought. He knew it was a friendly gesture in the human world, but he chose to take it as a wolf might in the wild, making the baring of her teeth a sign of aggression. *She's challenging me.*

He pushed himself harder.

Coach Quinn and the finish line were just ahead.

He was going to do it – Argus first, Shannon Boersma second.

But then he felt a presence on his left. Katelyn was there, sprinting toward the line.

Argus tried to match her speed. He kept pace for one . . . two . . . three strides, but she began to pull away.

Argus tried to push ahead, but he had nothing left. He coasted across the finish line more than a dozen feet behind.

Second. Not as bad as third, but again, he'd been beaten.

"Good run, Argus!" Coach Quinn applauded.

"Yeah, that was great," Shannon said. "You really pushed me hard at the end."

Argus did his best to be happy, but of course he wasn't. He'd come out to win. "Your little sister," he said, gasping for breath. "She beat me."

Shannon nodded. "Katelyn's a provincial champion in her age group. She's currently ranked third in the country."

"She made me come in second," Argus said, in disbelief.

"Yeah," Shannon said. "She was probably just playing with us."

By the time the rest of the team began to cross the line, Argus had caught his breath and was thinking about what he could do to improve himself for the next day. He'd run again tonight, of course, but running on the road wasn't the same as running through the forest. Cross-country running consisted of hills and valleys, uneven ground and the occasional obstacle to be avoided. The forest had all of those things. If he could run through the forest, then maybe he'd be better tomorrow.

Consumed by his thoughts, Argus headed back to the school before the rest of the team had finished the run.

"Argus?" Coach Quinn called. "Is everything okay?"

Argus kept walking.

"There's practice tomorrow," he said.

"I know," Argus said, without turning around. "I'll be there."

Chapter 11

The Redstone RCMP detachment was a small square building just off the main highway, at the south end of town. It was built of red brick in the 1970s, when the existing detachment was knocked down to make room for a supermarket. The lighted POLICE sign had been taken from the old building and looked its age. The tall rectangular windows and black-shingled roof had never been upgraded or repaired.

There were six empty parking spots out front, two to the left of the flagpole and four to the right. A Canadian flag flew at the top of the pole, with the RCMP standard flying beneath it. More parking spaces were around back, for police cruisers and people working inside, as well as a large garage door that allowed cars carrying prisoners to drive right into the building.

Ranger Brock was usually able to park out front whenever he visited the detachment, but today each of the spots was filled by an old pickup truck or beat-up car.

"Full house," he said, under his breath, as he drove around back. He parked his 4 x 4 in the spot furthest from the building. Then he exited his car and walked around to the front doors.

"Hi, Garrett," Mary Lou Valade said. She was the detachment's console operator, who took care of just about everything that didn't have to do with policing. Everyone called her Grammalou because she was never able to have a conversation without mentioning her grandchildren.

"Hey, Grammalou," he said, with a wave. "Are they here yet?"

She smiled and tilted her head backward. "Can't you hear them? They're making more noise than my grandkids on a Saturday night."

A slight din was coming from a room somewhere behind her. "You better get in there," she said. "The sergeant's been with them for twenty minutes and he's come out four times looking for you."

"Lead the way."

She got up from her desk and led him through the office to a meeting room at the back. As they got close, Garrett could hear the men all talking at once and felt his stomach tighten.

"Are you ready?" Grammalou asked, her hand on the doorknob.

"No," Garrett said.

"All right, then." She opened the door.

Suddenly, all the talking stopped. Everyone looked over at the open door.

Garrett stood there, sizing up the room. Ernie Ilson was there, of course, as were Terry Houghton from Redstone Lodge, Yvonne Nagleson from the riding stable, and Michael Bines, who represented local logging interests. Then there was Fatias Boyage, the hairdresser, who seemed a bit out of place in his knee-length overcoat and stylish fedora. No matter how diverse the crowd, everyone had a right to be there to voice their concerns.

Sergeant Martin was first to break the silence. "Ranger Brock, welcome," he said. "Hopefully you'll be able to answer questions better than I could."

"What's going on with that wolf I shot the other day?" Ernie Ilson asked, the anger in his voice unmistakable. "I heard that it ended up at your place and you called Doctor Katz to fix it up. That's not true, is it?"

"Afternoon, everyone," Garrett said, taking off his hat. "Why don't we all have a seat." He sat down and gestured for everyone else to do the same.

Ernie seemed in no mood for sitting. He put a knee on a chair and rested his hands on the table in the center of the room. "There, I'm sitting. Now tell me what the devil is going on."

Garrett took a deep breath. Finally he said, "It's true, the injured wolf did end up at my house and Doctor Katz was able to save it."

"Save it!" Ernie exclaimed. "What are you doing saving it when half the town is trying to kill it?"

The others in the room chimed in.

Garrett vowed to remain calm and professional. "Ladies and Gentlemen, I'm a forest ranger, a conservation officer for the Ministry of the Environment. It's my job to preserve wildlife and conserve our forests. I don't aid in the killing of wild animals. . . . I'm mandated to save and protect what I can."

"That wolf was one of the ones that took two of my rabbits and killed my dog. And other animals have gone missing too – dogs, cats, even chickens. You're helping the ones that did it. Please tell me you're doing something more than fixing up this wolf so it can kill again."

Garrett shook his head. "We're not caring for the wolf so it can kill again, but so we can move it far away from Redstone."

A collective groan filled the room.

"You're going to move it?" Terry Houghton said. "What's that going to do?"

"If we get the wolves far enough away from Redstone, they won't come back."

"How do you know that?" asked Fatias Boyage. "These wolves shouldn't be anywhere near Redstone to begin with, but here they are, not just on the outskirts of town, but right in town. So how can you guarantee us that there won't be any more blood spilled?"

Garrett wondered how he could know for sure what was in the mind of the werewolf behind his home and the other wolves in its pack. They were wild animals after all, and in the end, wild animals did whatever they wanted. But the werewolf leading this pack wasn't just a wild animal anymore, it was part human and had some of a human's ability to reason. It had brought the injured wolf to his home asking for help. It had sat silently behind his house, trusting the humans inside it to not harm the wolf. It had waited patiently for the wolf to heal. And the wave that Phyllis had called to tell him about had convinced Garrett that once the wolf had healed, they wouldn't be seeing the werewolf or its pack again.

He would have to tell these bloodthirsty, gun-toting barbarians just a bit of the truth and hope it would be enough.

"I just know," he said, at last.

Everyone began shouting at once.

"What?"

"You just know?"

"What's that suppose to mean?"

Garrett put up his hands. "You'll just have to trust me."

"You're crazy!" Ernie said. "Wolves are dangerous killers. They travel in packs. I shot *one*, and that means there are more out there. You can take this one wolf to the ends of the earth, but that's no guarantee that the others will follow it."

"But they will," Garrett said. "That pack have learned that Redstone is a dangerous place and they aren't going to come around here if they don't have to. . . ." But Garrett's voice was slowly drowned out by the shouts and cries of the other men in the room. They weren't interested in hearing about rehabilitation and conservation. They all wanted blood.

At last the sergeant stood up and called everyone to order. "That's enough!" he shouted, slamming a hand hard onto the table.

Moments later, everyone was silent.

"Now," the sergeant said, "I know that most of you have valid gun licenses and hunting permits, so I can't tell you to put your guns away and go about your business."

"Hell, yeah."

"That's right."

"So I'm warning you all here and now: If any of you hurts anybody, or shoots an animal out of season, or one that's protected by any municipal, provincial, or federal law, the full weight of the justice system will be brought down upon you. So you think about what the ranger has said, and then you decide if you want to give the man a chance to do his job, or if you'd like to take your chances with me."

Ernie Ilson gave a little laugh under his breath and shook his head. There were grumblings around the room, but the consensus was that they would give the ranger a couple of days to do it his way. Even so, both Garrett and the sergeant knew that if any other animals or livestock went missing, wolves – any wolves – would be fair game.

Satisfied, the sergeant called an end to the meeting. Everyone began filing out of the room.

"You think that did any good?" Garrett asked, when they were gone.

"I think most of them got it. Ernie Ilson's a tough nut to crack. I wouldn't be surprised if he still gives us some trouble."

Garrett then asked, "Which do you think are the more dangerous ones here, the humans or the wolves?"

The sergeant answered without hesitation. "Humans. Definitely humans."

Chapter 12

By the time Ernie Ilson got home later that afternoon, he'd had a lot of time to think about what Ranger Brock and Sergeant Martin had said about the pack of wolves terrorizing Redstone.

"They're crazy!" he spat, as he slammed the door behind him. "Both of them are doggone crazy!"

He took off his shoes and hung up his coat, then went to a cupboard in the kitchen where he kept two bottles of Canadian Club rye whiskey. He grabbed the fuller bottle and a large glass and headed for the living room.

"Don't get me wrong," he said to the empty house. "I'm all for saving the whales and all of that, but these wolves ain't no whales . . . and what's worse, they're here in my backyard."

He sat down in his favorite chair and poured himself a big stiff drink. As the rye whiskey splashed into the glass, Ernie instinctively looked down at the worn spot on the floor where Jaeger would have been – if he weren't dead.

He downed the whiskey in a single gulp, then poured himself another drink. "Those wolves are killers. Nothing but stone-cold killers. And that idiot ranger is trying to save one of them – fer what? So it can come back here and take another one of my rabbits, or someone else's dog?" He paused a moment, breathing deeply and seething with rage. He took another drink to calm his nerves, and this time he felt the fuzzy warmth of the whiskey start to cloud his head. "Damn government people. You have to wait until someone's killed before they'll do anything."

Ernie caught his breath. Again he looked down at the spot where his best friend, Jaeger, should have been. There were doggie toys strewn about, and a stain on the hardwood where Jaeger had thrown up a bowl of table scraps that hadn't agreed with him. He stared at the empty space for a long, long time until his eyes welled up with tears.

Uncapping the bottle of whiskey again, he tried to pour another glass, but his hand shook and he spilled most of the amber liquid. He stopped pouring, grabbed the bottle by the neck, and brought it to his lips. "I won't forget you, Jaeger." He took a swig from the bottle. "No matter what." One last swig. "And I won't let them get away with it, neither."

Ernie got up slowly from his chair, swaying slightly, then put on his coat. He slipped into his boots, pulled a tuque down hard onto his head, then picked up two things – the bottle of whiskey and his gun.

"They'll be back," he said, stumbling toward the door. "And when they come, I'll be ready for 'em."

He headed out to the edge of his property, the bottle in one hand, his gun in the other.

And waited. . . .

After dinner, Garrett and Phyllis left the dishes for the pack to clean and put away so they could head into Redstone. Janice Xia, a friend of Garrett's and a former ranger, had been accepted into the RCMP and there was a get-together for her at the Legion.

"You *will* clean the dishes, won't you?" said Phyllis, making the question sound like an order.

"Of course," answered Noble.

"And you have the number for the Legion in case you need to get in touch with us, right?"

Tora gestured with her head. "I can see it from here."

"And you'll keep an eye on the wolf out in the pen," said the ranger, as he stepped through the back door after checking up on it himself.

"Every thirty minutes," said Harlan.

"Do you think it's all right to leave her?" Phyllis asked the ranger.

"She'll be fine," the ranger said, with a smile. "It's not like we're leaving the animal alone. They're here, and we'll be back in a couple of hours."

"All right," Phyllis said, as if she still needed convincing.

"Besides, she's almost healed. My guess is she'll be wanting to leave sometime tonight or tomorrow, just like the doctor said."

"Then we won't stay too long tonight," Phyllis said, checking her watch.

"All right," the ranger replied, heading for the front door. "The sooner we get there, the sooner we can leave."

"See you guys later," Phyllis said, following the ranger out of the house.

Noble and Tora set to work clearing the dinner dishes off the table while Harlan filled the sink with dishwater. Everyone was working well together as a team.

Except for Argus.

"Where is Argus?" Tora asked, as she struggled with a heavy pile of plates.

Just then Argus appeared in the kitchen, wearing a hoodie, sweatpants, and sneakers.

Noble stopped what he was doing and said, "Where do you think you're going?"

"Running," said Argus.

"What? After the ranger clearly set the ground rules, you're still going running?"

Argus sighed. "I finished second today," he said.

"Great," said Harlan, "that's better than yesterday, right?"

"Second," Argus repeated, "as in the one that comes after the one who wins."

Noble wasn't getting it. "Yeah, so?"

"I want to win."

"You will win," Noble stated. "This is just training. In a week or two, you'll be running circles around everyone." A shrug. "Besides, who cares where you finish now? It's just practice."

"I care," Argus said.

Noble shook his head. "I can understand that you want to do well. But what's so important about winning?"

Argus tried to explain. "I'm the strongest of us four, right?"

Noble nodded, as did Tora and Harlan.

"And if we were a pack in the wild, I would be the alpha male, right?"

Noble had come to this conclusion years ago. In the wild, size and strength was everything and pack leaders were decided by fights – sometimes to the death – in order to find out who was strongest. But because the pack also lived in the human world, Argus knew he had to step aside and let Noble lead, something that had to bother him from time to time, like now.

"Here's something I can be number one at," Argus continued. "I can win, and all it'll take is practice."

"But what about what the ranger said?"

"He doesn't have to know. The ranger and Phyllis will be gone for at least two hours. I'll be back way before that."

It didn't sit right with Noble. "Look, the weekend's coming. We can all run with you . . . during the day."

Argus grinned. "That would be great. But I'm running tonight too." He headed for the front door.

"Argus. Don't!" was the last thing Noble said before his brother left the house.

Tora looked at Noble. "When is he ever going to learn?" she said.

"Not until something bad happens, I'm afraid."

Chapter 13

After they'd finished washing and putting away the dishes, there was a knock on the front door.

"Did Argus lock himself out?" Harlan asked, drying the last of the silverware – a misleading name for it since the knives and forks were all made out of stainless steel and the pack would never have anything made of silver in the house.

Noble took a look out the front window. "No, it's just Michael Martin."

"He didn't say anything about coming over," Tora said, a confused look on her face.

"Well, he's here," Noble said. "Don't leave him standing outside all night."

Tora answered the door. "Hi, Michael," she said.

"Hey!"

"What brings you here?" Tora asked.

"My bicycle."

"That's not what I meant."

Michael shrugged. "I don't know . . . I was in the area." A pause. "I haven't seen much of you lately and I was wondering if everything was okay."

Tora realized she'd been so wrapped up in her new friendship with Maria Abruzzo and engrossed by the plight of the werewolf in their backyard that it might have seemed like she'd forgotten all about her "boyfriend."

"C'mon in," she said, closing the door behind him.

"Hi, Michael," said Harlan.

"Hey, Mike," echoed Noble.

"He came to visit *me*," Tora said, grabbing him by the hand and leading him through the house to the back door.

"Where are we going?" he said.

"Out back. There's something I want to show you."

"Is it the wolf?" Michael asked.

"Yes," she said, grabbing her coat and slipping on her boots. "And more."

They stepped out the door and took the long way around the garage to the pen where the wolf was. She was up on all fours and moving about with a slight limp.

Tora crouched down behind a woodpile and gestured to Michael to do the same.

"What is it?" he said.

"Get down!"

Michael joined Tora and the two of them peered over the woodpile at the wolf. "Okay," he said. "What's the 'more' part?"

"Just wait."

They stayed there in silence, watching.

Then, with barely a sound, the werewolf came out of the forest and moved closer to the pen, until he was sitting at the fence with three fingers stretched straight through a hole in it. The wolf limped over and began rubbing her body against the fence.

"Wow!" said Michael. Tora had told him about the pack and their secret, but Michael had never really seen any of them in their full werewolf form.

"He's been out there waiting ever since he brought her here."

"Really? They must love each other."

They remained crouched behind the woodpile for the longest time, just watching the wolf and werewolf.

Finally Michael said, "So, this is what you've been doing with all your time lately. . . ." From the tone of his voice, it sounded as if he understood.

"I wonder," Tora said, "if I were hurt, would you wait for me like that?"

Michael didn't hesitate. "Of course. I'd visit you in the hospital every chance I got. Not only for you, but for your brothers too."

Tora smiled. Michael had been a great friend of the pack, helping them out even before he knew their secret. "That's nice to know," she said.

Michael shrugged. "You guys are the best friends I have."

Tora turned to him. "We're the *only* friends you have," she said, punching him playfully in the arm.

Ranger Brock and Phyllis returned from Redstone about twenty minutes after Michael Martin had gone home, but less than an hour after they'd left the house.

"How was the party?" Noble asked.

"The party was fine," Phyllis said, "but the ranger wanted to leave early."

"Why?" asked Tora.

"Everyone there wanted to know about the wolf," said the ranger. "I couldn't take three steps without someone asking me why I didn't let the wolf die, or telling me what I should have done instead."

Phyllis put a hand on his shoulder. "It wasn't much fun for him."

"So I said good-bye to Janice and left."

"It's probably just as well," Noble said. "I think it's time for you to let the wolf go."

"Why? What's happening?"

"You should see for yourself."

They all left the house, taking the long way around the garage and crouching low behind the woodpile so as not to startle the wolf and the werewolf.

The wolf was circling the inside of the pen. Each time she passed the werewolf, she would brush up against the fence and make a low whiny growl, the kind a dog might make when tied to a fence post waiting for its master.

The wolf wanted out.

The werewolf wanted her out too. It was picking at the fence with its talons, stretching the fencing and some of the holes, but not doing any real damage. There was no doubt the werewolf could tear a hole in the fence big enough for the wolf to escape, but it was holding off on that . . . for now.

"I'll call Doctor Katz," said the ranger.

He was gone for five minutes and when he came back, he had the key to the pen in his hand. "Doctor Katz says if the wolf's walking around, we should let her go. Her pack will take care of her the rest of the way."

"So this is it, then?" asked Phyllis.

The ranger nodded.

Phyllis put both hands against her cheeks. "This is so exciting . . . and romantic."

"I'd be happy if it were just *easy*," said the ranger.

He walked toward the pen's gate.

The werewolf moved away from the fence to the edge of the backyard, where it sat down and waited.

"What are you going to do?" Phyllis wanted to know.

"I'm going to open the pen and let her go, but first I want to make sure he's going to take his pack far away from here."

"How are you going to do that?"

"I don't know."

The ranger stood at the door to the pen, but did not open it. The wolf moved toward the door. When the door didn't open, she turned back and circled the pen.

"Come gather 'round me," said the ranger. "Let's show the werewolf I have a pack too."

They all stepped out from behind the woodpile – Phyllis taking a spot to the ranger's right; Harlan, Tora, and Noble taking up positions to his left.

The ranger looked around. "Where's Argus?"

"He went out," said Harlan.

"Where?"

"For a run."

The ranger was visibly upset by the news, but he didn't have time to dwell on it. "We'll deal with him later," he said. "Right now I've got to talk to a werewolf. Any suggestions?"

"Maybe it speaks English?" said Tora.

Harlan shook his head. "It's only been partly human for a few days. It couldn't possibly know the language already."

"And I'm no Dr. Dolittle," said the ranger.

"What about sign language?" Phyllis asked.

"I don't know sign language," responded the ranger.

The werewolf took several steps forward, halving the distance between them.

"Not real sign language," Phyllis said. "But maybe you could use hand signals and gestures to 'talk' to him."

"Worth a try, I guess," said the ranger.

He thought for a few moments, then said, "I'm Ranger Brock." As he said it, he placed an open hand on his chest. "Ranger Brock."

The werewolf watched, unmoving.

"And this is my pack." He pointed to the others.

The werewolf's eyes narrowed slightly, as if trying to understand.

"You," he said, pointing to the werewolf. Then he pointed to the wolves behind him in the forest. "Your pack."

The werewolf turned to look at the members of his pack, who had crept up to the edge of the forest to watch.

"So far so good," said Phyllis.

"I don't know," said the ranger.

"Keep going," said Noble. "I think you're making sense to him."

The ranger took a deep breath. "Me and my pack," he said, pointing to himself and the others, "we belong here." He gestured to the house, the garage, and the land in between.

He pointed to the werewolf and the wolves. "You and your pack . . . must go far away." He raised his bent right arm, then extended it to suggest a place well beyond the mountain. He repeated the motion several times, then, out of ideas, the ranger just stood there.

The werewolf took a step forward.

The ranger and Phyllis instinctively pulled back, while Noble, Tora, and Harlan partially changed their form to something between human and werewolf. If need be, at least they would be ready to defend the ranger and his wife.

But instead of lunging forward on the attack, the werewolf moved closer to the pen. Just a few feet from the gate, it began making hand gestures of its own.

"I think he's trying to communicate," squealed Tora.

Sure enough, the werewolf pointed to the wolf inside the pen.

"The wolf," said Phyllis.

Then he put an open hand over his chest, as Ranger Brock had done.

"And me, myself," said Harlan.

The werewolf clasped his hands tightly together.

"Are one?" said Noble.

"How about, belong together?" offered the ranger.

Again the werewolf put an open hand against his chest.

"I," said Phyllis.

A single finger pointed to the wolves in the forest behind him.

"And my pack," said Noble.

He then turned halfway toward the forest and pointed northward, as if he were pointing at something miles and miles away.

"Are going far away from here," Harlan guessed.

"Will be heading over the mountain," suggested the ranger.

Noble laughed. "Are getting the heck out of Redstone."

The werewolf indicated himself and his pack once more, then shook his head and crossed one hand over the other, like a referee calling off a play. Finally, he pointed straight down at the ground.

"I don't get it," said Tora.

"I think he's saying he doesn't belong here," said the ranger, "or that we won't be seeing him around here anymore."

He stepped over to the pen, slid the key into the lock, and opened the gate. Without a moment's hesitation, the wolf scampered out of the pen and joined the werewolf in the yard. The werewolf gave the wolf a long heartfelt hug. It was becoming more human with each passing day.

A second later, the wolf left the werewolf's side and went to join the other wolves still in the forest. They all rushed the wolf – rubbing, jumping, and licking – to welcome her back into the pack.

Alone once more, the werewolf rose up on its hind legs and stepped forward.

Again, the ranger tensed, unsure about what might happen.

The werewolf stopped directly in front of him, was still for a moment, then slowly outstretched its right hand.

"He wants to shake your hand," said Tora. "How does he know to do that?"

Ranger Brock thought about it, then said, "He must have seen me shake Doctor Katz's hand the other day and figured out it's a human custom."

"He learns fast," said Harlan.

"Well," said Phyllis. "Don't just stand there. Shake his hand."

Ranger Brock raised his right hand and placed it in the open hand of the werewolf. The ranger's hand settled into the lycanthrope's palm, reminding the ranger of the times when he'd held his father's hand as a child. Then, the werewolf curled his talons around the hand, making it almost disappear.

The ranger did his best to protect his hand from being crushed, but the werewolf was just too strong. He closed his hand tightly around the ranger's, almost breaking it with his vicelike grip.

The ranger tried to keep from crying out in pain, but his hand hurt too much. "*Ow!*" he cried.

Immediately the werewolf loosened its hold and turned to leave.

"I don't think he meant to hurt you," said Tora.

"No," said Phyllis. "He was just saying thank you."

"In that case, you're welcome," the ranger replied. His hand was red and swollen, and two of his fingers looked as if they might be broken.

The werewolf started to run across the yard and, within a few steps, changed from its full werewolf form to that of a wolf – a huge silver-gray wolf that couldn't seem to get into the forest fast enough.

Within seconds, it was racing north through the trees with the rest of its pack following close behind.

"Do you think that's the last we'll see of that wolf?" Phyllis asked.

The ranger massaged his swollen hand. "I hope so," he said. "For my sake . . . and the sake of the town."

Just then, the report of a gunshot echoed off the mountain.

"What was that?" asked Tora.

"Somebody's shooting," replied Noble.

"Oh, no," said the ranger. "Not again."

Chapter 14

Ranger Brock was busy on the house phone trying to get hold of Sergeant Martin, or anyone else at the RCMP detachment, to find out what was going on. His first concern was for who or what had been shot. He doubted it was a wolf since all of the wolves of the werewolf's pack had been in the forest behind the house when the shot was fired. Chances that it was another wolf or wild animal were slim. That left a human target, and few people roamed the forests around Redstone after dark. . . .

The front door opened and in stepped Noble.

"Did you find him?" Phyllis asked.

Noble shook his head. He'd been down to the main highway, searching about a half-mile in each direction.

Outside, Tora and Harlan were returning from a quick search of the forest behind the house. Phyllis went to the back door to meet them. "Any luck?" she asked.

"No," said Tora. "There was no sign of Argus anywhere, but we did follow the trail of the wolves for a while."

"They headed due north," said Harlan. "Just like he said they would."

Phyllis smiled bravely. "That's one less thing to worry about." She held the door open for Tora and Harlan as they entered the house.

Just then, the ranger's cell phone began to buzz, where it sat on the hall table by the front door. With the ranger on the house phone in the kitchen, Phyllis rushed over and picked it up.

"Hello?" she said, unable to mask the panic in her voice.

"Hi, Phyllis," the familiar voice replied.

"Sergeant Martin. Garrett's been trying to get hold of you."

"Well, if he'd get off the phone for a minute, maybe he'd receive a call or two."

"We heard the shot," she said. "And Argus should have been home by now –"

"It's him," the sergeant said, without hesitation.

The words hit Phyllis like a hard punch to the stomach. "What?"

"Argus," said the sergeant. "He was the one who was shot."

Phyllis began waving frantically at the ranger to hang up the phone and listen to the sergeant on the cell.

"How bad is he hurt?"

The ranger joined her, leaning in close so he could hear the sergeant.

"He was shot in the leg at fairly close range. Lucky for him, Ernie Ilson had been drinking and his aim was off. If he'd been sober . . ."

"So you've seen Argus?" asked the ranger.

"Of course I've seen him," answered the sergeant.

"The wound, I mean. You've seen it?"

"Yeah, but why's that important?"

The ranger already knew Argus would be all right. What he wanted to know was whether or not Argus had tried to speed up the healing process by changing his form from human to wolf and back again. "I just want to know . . . if he'll be all right."

"Well," began the sergeant. "His leg was bleeding pretty bad at first, but the doctor patched him up and said he should be fine, except he won't be doing any more running for a while."

"That's good news," said the ranger.

"Very good news," echoed Phyllis, on the verge of tears.

After a pause, Garrett said, "I'm wondering if you could do me a favor."

"Anything, of course."

"I want you to stay with Argus until I get there."

"Will do."

"And don't let him out of your sight for a minute."

"Okay, I get it," the sergeant said, a little annoyed. It was, after all, a pretty straightforward request.

"Thank you, we'll be right there."

They were at the hospital a little over a half hour later. It was well after dark, and an icy chill seemed to hang in the air, biting through their clothes as they got out of the car.

Noble ran across the parking lot, leaving the others behind. He wanted to speak to Argus alone for a few moments.

There were people from town in the lobby, mostly the family and friends of those being treated at the hospital. One person who seemed out of place there was Ernie Ilson, sitting in a chair by the vending machine in the waiting area. An RCMP officer was sitting in the seat next to him.

Noble poked his head into Argus's room and saw Sergeant Martin on a chair next to the bed.

"Hello, Noble," he said. "Where's your father?"

"Right behind me," Noble replied.

"Good," said the sergeant. "I want to talk to him." He got up from his chair. "Do me a favor and watch your brother for a minute. Your father doesn't want him to be alone."

"No problem," Noble said, smiling.

Noble watched the sergeant leave the room, then rushed to Argus's bedside. With any luck, the ranger and Phyllis would be tied up for a few minutes by people outside Argus's room.

"How are you?" Noble asked.

"I got shot." Argus said.

"What were you thinking. . . ," Noble asked, with a slight shake of his head, "running through the forest like that?"

Argus sighed.

"The ranger allowed you to go running along the main roads. What were you doing in the woods?"

Another sigh. "It felt good to run – even as a human on the side of the road – so I just kept running. I didn't care where I was, or how far I'd gone. Before I knew it, I was halfway around the mountain and it was getting dark. If I came back on the road, who knows what time I would have returned. So I took a shortcut –"

"Through the woods?"

"Through the woods. Right by Ernie Ilson's place." Argus shook his head as if he knew it was a stupid thing to do.

"The ranger's pretty angry. I think he's disappointed in you, too."

"I can imagine," replied Argus. "I'm more worried about facing him and what he's going to say than I am about being shot."

"Does it hurt?"

"A little." Argus shifted on the bed. "The sergeant's been with me the whole time, so I haven't had a chance to heal yet. If you watch the door for me, I could change form a few times and be able to leave the hospital tonight."

"No way," Noble said. "I'm not going to help you do that."

"Why not?" Argus said, his eyes wide.

"Because I told him not to. . . ," the ranger said, entering the room, followed by Phyllis, Tora, and Harlan.

Argus's body sank back into the bed and he pulled the covers up tight over his shoulders.

"And unlike you," the ranger continued, "Noble has no problem following my instructions."

He stopped at Argus's bedside and glared at him a moment. Then he pulled back the covers to see Argus's leg. The wound was midway on the thigh. There was a large white dressing around the leg, with a red splotch in the middle of it the size of a dinner plate. He pulled the sheets back over Argus. "I allowed you to join the cross-country running team, and you used that as an excuse to go running in the evening."

"But I –" Argus said, before being cut off by the ranger's firm raised hand.

"Then I allowed you to run on the roads, and you used that as an excuse to go running through the forest."

Argus lowered his eyes and looked at the floor.

"I gave you a leaf; you took the branch. I gave you a branch; you tried to take the whole tree."

"Yes, Ranger," Argus said, the tone of his voice leaving no doubt that he understood that what he'd done was wrong.

"You openly defied me, and now you're going to have to accept the consequences. You are going to suffer through your recovery *as a human.* No shape-shifting, no changing form. Is that understood?"

"That means the cross-country season will be over by the time I'm healed."

"That's right," said the ranger. "No more running for you for a while. Part of it is punishment, the rest is to save your life."

"Yes, Ranger."

The ranger sighed, uncomfortable with disciplining Argus by taking away the thing he loved most. He looked at Argus again, his eyes softer now. "Did you know that the gunsmith in town has been busy the past few days making silver bullets and peppering buckshot with bits of silverware and old coins?"

Argus's face turned white.

Noble could feel the blood drain away from his face too. With the citizens of Redstone armed with silver-laced ammunition, a wound from any one of those rounds would have been fatal to any member of the pack.

"When I forbid you to do something, there's a reason for it. That's why I expect my instructions to be obeyed."

Phyllis stepped forward then, putting a hand on the ranger's arm. "I think he understands."

Argus nodded. "I'm sorry," he said, "for going against your wishes and for almost getting myself killed."

"Fine," the ranger said. Then he smiled. "Just don't do it again."

When Ranger Brock left the hospital room, he found Sergeant Martin waiting in the lobby, along with Ernie Ilson. It would take time, but Argus would heal from his wounds and eventually be as good as ever. In addition, he'd learned a valuable lesson through this whole ordeal.

But despite the positive outcome for the pack, there was still the matter of Ernie Ilson and his redneck "brothers." Just because the wolf was gone and Argus shot didn't mean the matter was over.

"How's he taking it?" asked the sergeant, as he got up to meet the ranger.

"He'll live," answered the ranger.

"Strong boy you've got there. Lucky, too. The way this wolf scare has gotten everyone so nervous, it's a wonder he wasn't killed."

"I told him as much."

The ranger nodded his head in the direction of Ernie Ilson, then asked, "What are you going to do about him?"

"I've been giving that some thought. He knows he's in a lot of trouble, and he feels terrible shooting Argus."

"Can you charge him?"

"That's just the thing," said the sergeant. "He's got a permit for the gun and a license to hunt. It would be pretty hard to prove he shot Argus on purpose."

"I understand," said the ranger.

"The best I can do is something like careless use of a firearm, but even that would be tough since he was still a pretty good shot, even if he was drunk."

Ranger Brock turned slightly so that his back was to the old man still sitting in one of the waiting-room chairs. "Does he know there's really nothing you can charge him with?"

"No," the sergeant said, with a curious smile. "He thinks I'm waiting to drop the hammer on him."

"How about. . . ," the ranger began, "how about you let him off with a warning and use this whole incident to convince everyone else in town that it's best to put away their guns before somebody *does* get killed."

"I can do that." Then he shook his head. "But what does it say about the people in this town when someone has to be shot, and nearly killed, before they consider putting away their guns?"

The ranger shrugged. "I don't know, but whatever it says about them, it can't be good."

When they turned to face Ernie Ilson, the sergeant whispered to Ranger Brock, "Follow my lead. Maybe we can scare him into helping us."

Ernie saw them looking his way and suddenly stood up, his hat in his hands. "I'm sorry, Ranger Brock. I never meant to hurt your son. . . . I thought he was one of them wolves. Honest to God, I did."

Ranger Brock had no trouble believing him. But that didn't mean he was going to let him off easy. "Crazy old man, you're lucky you didn't kill him."

"I know, I know," Ernie said. "I've already put away that gun and locked it up good. I won't be shootin' anything for a long while, 'cept maybe a game of pool."

"Sorry to tell you, Ernie," the sergeant said, "but there aren't any pool tables in jail."

"What?" Ernie's eyes grew as big as headlights. "You can't put me in jail. I already told you, I didn't mean to hurt the boy. I thought he was a wolf and I was defending my property."

The sergeant looked Ernie in the eye. "I didn't necessarily say I was putting you in jail . . . but I am thinking about it."

"What's jail going to do for an old man like me? I made a mistake, sure, but I can guarantee you I won't never make the same mistake again."

Ranger Brock snapped his fingers like he'd been thinking hard and the answer just occurred to him.

"What is it?" answered the sergeant.

"What if instead of charging Ernie with something like attempted murder, or assault with a weapon, we call one last town meeting so *he* can tell everyone how wrong he was about wanting to kill the wolves? He could even suggest that everyone should put away their guns. . . ."

"I can do that," Ernie said. "I won a prize for public speaking in elementary school, you know. I could tell everybody that guns is the wrong way to go, and then I could even make sure they put down their weapons. I can do that for you, easy."

The sergeant stroked his chin like he was considering the offer. "I don't know."

"Gimme a chance, Sarge," Ernie said. "I won't let you down."

"Everyone should get a second chance," said Ranger Brock.

"Okay," the sergeant said, at last. "You convince everyone to stop shooting and I won't put you in jail."

"Oh, thank you, thank you," Ernie said, shaking first the sergeant's hand, then the ranger's. "And you tell your son no hard feelings, okay? He won't have to worry about me hurtin' him ever again."

"That's good," said the ranger. "I'll let him know . . . and I'll tell him not to kill you when he gets out of the hospital."

"What?" Ernie's face went white.

"Relax," the ranger said, "that was a joke."

"Oh, yeah?" Ernie said, gasping for breath.

"Argus would never kill you. He'd only beat you to within an inch of your life."

"Really?" You could almost feel the fear in Ernie's voice.

"No, not really." A pause. "That was another joke."

Ernie sighed. "Oh."

"C'mon," said the sergeant. "Let's get him out to my car before we have to carry him there."

Chapter 15

It was late afternoon the next day when Harlan and Noble went to visit their bigger brother at the hospital. On the way, Harlan picked up a fresh hot burger and an order of french fries at the drive-in restaurant next to the school. Although the hospital was feeding Argus three meals a day, Harlan was sure Argus wasn't getting half as much food as he needed.

"Hey, brother," Harlan said, as he entered the room.

"How you doing, Argus?" Noble asked.

Argus sniffed the air. "Am I smelling what I think I'm smelling?"

"You are," Harlan said, placing the greasy brown-paper bag on the bed.

Argus grabbed it and began wolfing down the burger. He was four or five bites into it before he noticed that Harlan was dressed in running shoes, sweats, and a school T-shirt.

"Why are you dressed like that?" Argus asked, around a bite of burger.

"Well," Harlan began. "Since you're not on the cross-country team anymore, Coach Quinn asked me if I wanted to run in your place."

"What? You took *my* spot on the team?"

"Not really. Anyone who wants to can join the team. And by the time you're out of the hospital and well enough to run, the cross-country season will be over."

Argus just looked at Harlan. "But you're so . . . well, skinny. There are some fast people on that team, especially Shannon Boersma's younger sister, Katelyn. I just couldn't catch her. How are you going to do against someone like that?"

Noble put a hand over his mouth to try and hide his laugh.

"What's so funny?" Argus said.

"Uh," Harlan began. "I don't know how to tell you this, but I ran with the team today."

"Yeah, and?"

"Well, I finished first."

"No way!"

Harlan shrugged. "It's just practice."

"You finished ahead of Katelyn?"

Harlan nodded.

"She's a provincial champion."

"I know. Coach Quinn was really impressed."

"*Impressed*," said Noble, looking at Harlan. "He was practically doing handstands."

"There's a meet next weekend," said Harlan. "He's expecting me to win."

Argus's whole body slumped forward, his chin coming to rest on his chest.

Noble felt a little sorry for his brother. Harlan just happened to be the slowest member of the pack in their wolfen form. But if Argus was angry, he let it pass.

Argus raised his head. "Maybe I'll be out in time to watch you run."

"That would be nice," said Harlan.

Noble had trouble believing what he was hearing. He looked into Argus's eyes and said, "What have you done with our brother?"

"I'm still me," Argus said. "But I figure, if it's not me leading the running team, at least it'll be a Brock." He extended his hand in Harlan's direction.

"Thanks, Argus," Harlan said, shaking it. "It means a lot to me that you feel that way."

"I'm glad you're taking this so well, Argus," Noble said. "Because we've got another little surprise for you."

"What?" Argus asked, smiling. "What is it?"

Noble reached into his backpack and pulled out a textbook and two notebooks.

Argus's smile was gone in an instant. "What's this?"

"When Mr. Surujpaul heard you were going to be in the hospital for a few days, he sent these books along. He felt that lying in bed would be the perfect opportunity for you to brush up on your math and improve your mark."

He put the books on Argus's bed.

"But my math mark has been okay."

Noble shook his head. "Mr. Surujpaul knows you've been copying people's work and cheating on tests. He said this will give you the chance to catch up to everyone else."

"I hate math," Argus said.

"Otherwise," Noble continued, "he'll have to talk to the ranger about you."

"But I'm willing to learn."

"That's good to know," Noble said, putting a hand on his brother's shoulder. "I'll be sure to tell Mr. Surujpaul."

Argus took the textbook and cracked it open to the first chapter. "Who wants to help me study?"

Harlan let out a nervous laugh. "I'd love to, but now that I'm on the cross-country team," a shrug, "I gotta run."

With that, Harlan hurried out of the room.

Argus stared at the doorway, wishing he were running out of the hospital with Harlan.

"Don't worry, brother," Noble said. "I'll stay and study with you. After all, misery loves company, and I hate math just as much as you do."

Later that night, Friday night, the air was filled with the delicious smell of pizza baking in Mr. Gusto's oven. Both Maria and Tora were there, along with Michael Martin, Harlan and Noble, and Maria's younger sister, Angelina.

They'd just ordered a party-sized pizza – one-third triple cheese, one-third vegetarian, and one-third meat lovers – when Gabriela Santos and her friend Irene Horne walked into the restaurant.

Maria's eyes went wide in surprise. "I thought you were busy tonight," she said.

"I am," Gabriela said.

"Doing what?"

"Having a pizza and seeing a movie with my friends."

"But that's what *we're* doing," Maria said. "Why don't we do it together?"

The girls laughed at Maria. Gabriela pointed to Tora, Harlan, and Noble. "*They're* not our friends."

"They're weird," Irene said.

"But they're my friends now. That makes them your friends too."

"Really," Gabriela said. "You used to call Tora a mutt and the rest of them hairy monsters. Now, all of a sudden, they're your friends?"

Maria looked awkwardly at Tora and the others. "You're right," she said. "After everything I did and said to them, I can't believe they're my friends either, but they are." She took a deep breath. "I've admitted many times now that it was wrong for me to act the way I did. But, more importantly, I've apologized and they've forgiven me. If that's not friendship, what is?"

Gabriela crossed her arms over her chest. "They just want to be your friend so they can be cool."

Noble laughed out loud at that, as did Harlan and Michael Martin. Tora managed only a slight smile, making Noble wonder if she thought what the girl had said was partly true.

Maria shook her head. "No, I don't think they do anything just to be cool." Then she turned to Gabriela and Irene. "Like when my sister went missing," she said, pointing a finger. "Where were you guys?"

"Yeah," said Angelina. "Where were you?"

"I had dance class," said one.

"My brother had a hockey game," said the other.

"Right," said Maria. "Well, they spent the night in the woods looking for her, and they ended up saving her life. How could I not be their friend after that?"

"But look at them," said Gabriela. "They're . . . *weird*."

This time Maria didn't even bat an eye. "They're not weird, they're *different*. And that's what makes them such great people. Such good friends."

Noble felt pride swelling in his chest. No one had ever said such kind things about the pack, and certainly not in such a public place. He appreciated Maria's new friendship, but now he had an admiration for her too.

Irene looked confused. "Maria, what have they done to you? You used to hate them so much."

Maria ignored the comment. "Look," she said. "Don't make me choose between you and them. You either accept them as *your* friends because they're *my* friends, or you can just give me back all the stuff you've *borrowed* from me over the years."

Noble watched with rapt fascination. Maria had been so forceful, so adamant, that there was no longer any question where her loyalties lay.

Finally, Gabriela said, "You're going to see *Wolf Hounds of Death Creek* tonight, right?"

"That's right," Maria said, her voice even and unflinching.

"Well, I guess it wouldn't hurt if we all saw it together. I mean, as a group."

Maria smiled, then grabbed a chair from a nearby table. "We've ordered a party-sized pizza. You're welcome to have some with us, if you like."

The two girls sat down. Then, Gabriela said, "That's a nice blouse, Tora."

"Thanks," Tora said, smiling. "I borrowed it from Maria."

Everyone laughed.

Noble leaned over and tugged on Maria's shirt sleeve. "Thank you," he said.

"For what?"

Noble thought about what to say, but he didn't know quite how to put it.

"Thank you," he said, at last. "For being our friend."

Acknowledgments

I'd like to thank the following people for lending their names to a worthy cause – Ron Camacho, Erin McMillan, Ayris Oakland, Brian Hewlitt (and his dogs, Jaeger and Hanna), Yvonne Nagleson, Noel Nagleson, Terry Houghton, Halina Houghton, Kyan Houghton, Spencer Houghton, Daniel Colp, Gabriela M. Santos, Mary Lou Valade, Leon Surujpaul, Shannon Boersma, Katelyn Boersma, and Terry Magill. I'd also like to thank my wife, Roberta, without whose love and support the writing of this book, or any other, would not have been possible.

About the Author

Wolf Man is the fourth novel in the Wolf Pack saga, which began with *Wolf Pack* (winner of the Aurora and Silver Birch Awards), and continued in the pages of *Lone Wolf* and *Cry Wolf*. In addition to writing about the wolf pack, Edo van Belkom has edited two collections of stories for young readers, *Be Afraid!* and *Be Very Afraid!*, and published more than 220 short stories, as well as dozens of other books of mystery, fantasy, and horror. Born in Toronto, Edo has worked as everything from school bus driver to newspaper reporter, television movie host to prisoner escort officer. He currently lives in Brampton, Ontario, with his wife and son.

Praise for the work of EDO VAN BELKOM

WOLF PACK

Winner, 2005 Aurora Award

Winner, 2006 Silver Birch Award

"Van Belkom knows how to blend the real-life world of adolescence with the dark possibilities afforded by fiction. Exciting."

– St. Catharines Standard

LONE WOLF

Nominee, 2006 Aurora Award

"It is unusual for a sequel to be even as good as an original novel, and it's even rarer for it to be better, but that's the situation with LONE WOLF*, the sequel to* WOLF PACK*."*

– CM Magazine

CRY WOLF

". . . story is full of action, but also interesting bits of character development. . . . Let's hear it for the werewolves!"

– CM Magazine

"CRY WOLF *is a fast-paced and straightforward read, which will appeal both to younger readers and to high school students who are not yet reading at an adult level . . . the story is well-told and the writing is never condescending . . . the heroes are likeable and believable."*

– Resource Links